The Easy Life

ALSO BY MARGUERITE DURAS

The Impudent Ones

The Lover

The North China Lover

The Ravishing of Lol Stein

The Sailor from Gibraltar

The Vice-Consul

The War: A Memoir

L'Amante Anglaise

Blue Eyes, Black Hair

Emily L.

Four Novels

Green Eyes

Hiroshima, Mon Amour

India Song

The Little Horses of Tarquinia

The Malady of Death

Outside: Selected Writings

Practicalities

The Sea Wall

Yann Andrea Steiner

Summer Rain

Destroy, She Said

No More

The Man Sitting in the Corridor

Whole Days in the Trees

The Atlantic Man

The Slut of the Normandy Coast

Eden Cinema

The Easy Life

Marguerite Duras

Translated by Emma Ramadan and Olivia Baes

BLOOMSBURY PUBLISHING
NEW YORK • LONDON • OXFORD • NEW DELHI • SYDNEY

BLOOMSBURY PUBLISHING
Bloomsbury Publishing Inc.
1385 Broadway, New York, NY 10018, USA

First published in the United States 2022

LIBRARY OF CONGRESS CATALOGING-IN-PUBLICATION DATA IS AVAILABLE

ISBN: TPB: 978-1-63557-851-5; eBook: 978-1-63557-852-2

2 4 6 8 10 9 7 5 3 1

Typeset by Westchester Publishing Services
Printed and bound in the U.S.A.

For my mother

FOREWORD

Everyone Says You Were Beautiful When You Were Young

The silence that must fall when the baby naps, still on me. The stack of Marguerite Duras books on the couch, a slim paper notebook. I reread *The Lover,* written when Duras was seventy, which I've read countless times, then *The Easy Life,* the first translation in English of her second novel, written in her twenties, which is new to me. I take notes on Duras with my breast still out. The baby's father and her sister are in the kitchen, making hot chocolate, tofu for soup. It is February. There was just a snow squall—heavy winds, snow falling like paper.

Besides her nap, which lasts only an hour, two at the most, the baby has not been sleeping. It's unbelievable, this sleep regression. She wakes up every two hours in the night; I contort my body, give her my breast. She refuses the crib. In the morning her father lets me sleep for an hour, the way I did as a child, on my stomach, one leg hitched up, the other stretched diagonally across, comforter curled around me, the utter abandonment of this, of the way I used to be allowed to sleep.

I wake up to the children mewing like cats.

How tired I am. The fatigue is almost gilded. I pass by the bathroom mirror. I see myself as a smeared woman. My exhaustion makes me ancient. My face has completely fallen. Later while allowing myself a break, I will look up inexpensive eyelash curlers, as I have read that it might make my eyes look more awake. I order one online.

There is that photograph of Marie Legrand, the mother of Marguerite Donnadieu (before she changed her last name to Duras, the town of her father's birth, when she published her first novel). Her mother who dresses as a widow or a nun, face lined and tired, her hair in a bun. She is surrounded by her three children, a four-year-old Marguerite, her two older brothers. Tiny Marguerite has an old woman's face. They all have the same face. Funny how family does this. Reading *The Lover* this time, I recognize the deep fatigue of the mother. How she manages to clothe her children. How her children are constantly outgrowing their shoes, the gold heels subbing in for the regular white canvas shoes that could get filthy, definitely purchased on final markdown. Duras writes these early scenes in *The Lover* as someone who has been someone's mother as well. Even in *The Easy Life*, the narrator takes care of her baby nephew, the beautifully strange passage of him suckling on her, of the tenderness and brutality of caretaking. "The suction sound he made while suckling, so slight, revealed to me that I had a body that was still very young despite my thick and ancient fatigue. I felt it coursing with a series of shivers so new, so morning-like, that I laughed to myself." My morning before being on the couch, reading Duras, I go through bags of clothes, trying to see what hand-me-downs will fit the baby in the coming months, what T-shirts and shorts will fit my five-year old's lengthening body. Their metallic sneakers they are so proud of, purchased on deep discount, are getting too snug. The strange atmosphere of this February—a sudden sixty-degree day, we blink with everything so bright, remember that spring will come eventually, and then this snow squall.

This might be the photograph of her mother's despair, which Duras writes about in *The Lover*, taken in the courtyard in front of the house in Hanoi, the inability for the single mother sometimes to clothe or feed them. As she looks at it, from the vantage of old age, Duras does not know who took this photograph. The mother—a category so rarely photographed.

The surprise again, looking at this photograph, realizing my mother also had three young children in the house. That she did the best she could. That I couldn't be easily controlled. That she had no help. Already I fight with the five-year-old. Her moods and rages. She complains we favor the baby, give her all the attention. She has barricaded herself inside her room, the room that used to be my office, with her private rituals and ceremonies. At night we come together again, I hold her, braid her hair, so it doesn't tangle, just like the mother of *The North China Lover*, written at the end of Duras's life, a retelling again of her childhood in colonial Vietnam. I braid my daughter's hair at night—silently. In the morning she jumps in my lap and tells me her dreams. I am the mother, not the girl. When reading of the family romance of Duras in all its endless variations, begun with the first novels, so marked in *The Easy Life*, I think of the three of us small children, the exhaustion and tenderness my mother still no doubt felt for me, even though I was not the favored young brother who could do no wrong.

There is that moment in *The North China Lover* where the mother of the young narrator wakes up, for a moment, and looks at her—really looks at her with a tender curiosity. There is a variation on conversations recounted between the mother and daughter in *The Lover.* The mother's desire for the daughter to pursue mathematics, or business. The daughter wants to become a writer. What will you write about when you write your books? the mother asks. Paolo, she says. You. And Pierre, just so I can kill him off. Her mother, and her two brothers. The family romance. Why, the young girl protests, do you love him so much more than us? The mother cuts her off, lies: I love my three children the same. Earlier in the conversation, the daughter worries over her older brother's brutality, that he might kill his younger brother. They are always fighting, like Cain and Abel. Here, and in *The Lover,* it is clear she becomes a writer because of this family, to try to understand them, their poverty, their cruelty, their violence, to try to understand this exclusion.

When she is eighty, possibly while collecting her meditations on writing in *Écrire*, Duras goes back and rereads this second novel, ironically titled *La vie tranquille,* translated here as *The Easy Life*. It was written a year after her first novel, both set not in French Indochina but in Duras country, the rural southwest of France, where her father was from and where she spent some time as an adolescent at the estate he purchased right before his untimely death, a novel of what she called later "boundless childhood," of family melodrama. This second novel was written in 1943 and published one year later, at the end of 1944, the first to be published by the prestigious publisher Gallimard. Her husband Robert Antelme was still a prisoner at Buchenwald then, having been a part of the resistance as was she. The novel was written one year after the death of her beloved younger brother Pierre, just months after her child was stillborn. The incredible pain that made her desire to stop existing, and also made her a writer, as if to write out of this despair, what Duras called *douleur.*

In 1993, when she read *The Easy Life* again, Duras remembered that it poured out of her while writing, as if in one breath, in the "very banal and dark logic of a murder." She is impressed by this work, by its intensity, by the force in which it came out of her. This is the first work in which she writes about a desire to murder a brother figure, which she writes about in so much depth later on in *The Lover,* a novel about the desire to write, and to write her way out of the family, but it begins here, in *The Easy Life*, along with other marks of Durassian style. Here, the first of many variations on a mother figure, a codependent and brutal older son, a beloved other brother, the tragedy of brother figures and family ties. In *The Lover,* she writes, "I wanted to kill my elder brother, I wanted to kill him, to get the better of him for once, just once, and see him die."

The book is about a murder, one of three deaths, all of men. It is divided in three parts. The longest part of the book, over an eternal August, tracks the elongated death scene and wake of the at once hated and loved uncle of Françoise, killed in an act of vengeance by her brother, at her provocation. Françoise is twenty-six, the same age that the author was while writing it, distinct from the memory theater of the later works. What follows, over almost a hundred pages, is the "chaos, boredom, chaos" of rural life, a surreal pastoral of animals and mythical woods, love triangles, including with the adored brother, who here is younger, and a set of parents, farm workers, including a father brought back from the dead, and one of the first of mythical Maman figures, who mostly lie around in bed, silent. Although in this novel the style that has been called *dépouillée*—the naked, stripped-down, spoken-voice quality of the later works—isn't as pronounced, there is still the classic atmosphere of lassitude here, and especially later on, a disorientation, the rhythm of an existential crisis that we can recognize as Durassian, as well as flights of her wild lyricism, as translated by Emma Ramadan and Olivia Baes:

> I was no one, I had neither name nor face. Moving through August, I was: nothing. My steps made no sound, nothing signaled that I was there, I disturbed nothing. At the bottom of the ravines, frogs full of life croaked, educated in August things, death things.

Here there is, off scene, the suicide of the brother, and then the deep melancholic boredom and *douleur* that results as the narrator, who we recognize even more in the second part as a variation on a Duras woman, takes off for the coastal town of T. in order to contemplate her borderless grief, to contemplate the endless sea. This noirish spirit of convalescence with an aloof woman narrator now reminiscent of *Destroy, She Said* or *The Malady of Death*. There is the incidental character of a bothersome candy salesman who she later witnesses drowning, leading her to be expelled from the cheap hotel at which she's staying, but any attempt at action, to shoehorn this into a more conventional novel, feels artificial compared to the pull of the sea, of exquisite boredom and absurdity, the woman's body passive in the sand. The reading report of Raymond Queneau, who rejected the first novel at Gallimard, critiqued a "muddled narrative" and a "lack of control" in *La vie tranquille*, but Gallimard published it anyway, finding here a true writer's voice. Surely this fails in being a more successful, conventional novel, culminating in an italicized, feverish return and even a marriage plot. And yet it is the loss of control of the Duras narrator and her writing of her narrative that is the point, a breaking down that will become her trademark in later works—the instability of point of view, of her sense of self, a woman alone in a room, staring at a mirror, attempting to both disappear and find herself, calling her fragmentation and a fragmented voice into existence.

I find myself, upon rereading *The Lover*, irritated by the man at the opening who tells the narrator, now elderly, that he likes her face as it is now, ravaged. *Everyone says you were beautiful when you were young.* Reading it this time, I feel even more deeply how both *The Easy Life* and *The Lover* are meditations on vanity and aging, on faces, on this currency that the Duras narrator exchanges for being able to write her own narrative. Her face, she tells us in *The Lover*, in this constant conversation with the reader, took on a new appearance at eighteen, between eighteen and twenty-five, the age in which she began to write novels. She watched this process of her face, like reading a book, the book of her life. She stopped being able to recognize herself then, herself as a child, and it was this distance, perhaps, that allowed her to begin writing. Also alienated from her family, one of her brothers dead, she has the space to write herself into each book, transforming herself along the way.

There is a photograph of myself in my late twenties. Cross-legged on a chair in a London flat, where we were staying with a friend. Exhausted from jetlag. Circles under my eyes like bruises. I think of this photograph, in my mind, I don't know where there's a copy, of my first real photograph as a writer.

The suddenness of Francine's aging is the true story of *The Easy Life*. In the hotel room, she finds herself staring at a mirror, in an extraordinary passage of existential crisis, seeing herself in the third person as if for the first time, all of the endless variations of her that she might write someday, even thirty years from now. And we know that she does. "Here, in my room, it's me. It's as if she no longer knows it's her."

—Kate Zambreno
Brooklyn, New York
February 2022

The Easy Life

PART ONE

Jérôme walked back to Les Bugues broken in two. I joined Nicolas, who had sprawled out on the railway embankment after the fight. I sat down next to him, but I don't think he even noticed. He watched Jérôme until the path disappeared into the woods. Then Nicolas rose in a hurry and we ran to catch up with our uncle. As soon as we saw him again, we eased our pace. We walked about twenty meters behind him and just as slowly.

Nicolas was all sweaty. His hair was sticky and fell in strands across his face; his chest was heaving and marked with red and purple blotches. The sweat trickled from his armpits, in drops, along his arms. He continued to watch Jérôme with extraordinary focus. At that moment, beyond my uncle's hunched back, Nicolas must have glimpsed everything that was to come.

The path to Les Bugues is steep. From time to time Jérôme would lean against the embankment, folded over himself, both hands pressed to his side.

At some point, he noticed us behind him but didn't seem to recognize us. He was clearly suffering a great deal.

Nicolas, right beside me, was still watching him. A series of images must have been triggered inside him, images unfolding, unfolding, always the same ones, and he was unable to break free from his surprise. He probably thought it was still possible to undo what he had done, and his hands, red and sweaty, clenched.

Every twenty meters Jérôme leaned against the embankment. He didn't care anymore that Nicolas had struck him. Nicolas or anyone. His face now expressed neither the rage nor the vexation from earlier, when Nicolas had gone to get him out of bed. He had swallowed himself, it seemed, and was watching himself from the inside, dazzled by his own suffering. It must have been terrible. He seemed to find it impossible, to have trouble believing it.

From time to time he tried to stand back up and a huff of stupor slipped from his chest. Along with these moans, something foamy came out of his mouth. His teeth chattered. He had completely forgotten us. He was no longer counting on us to help him.

It was Tiène who gave me these details after Nicolas told him the story later on. In the moment, I was watching my brother.

For the first time, I saw greatness in my brother Nicolas. His warmth left his body as vapor and I could smell his sweat. It was Nicolas's new scent. He looked only at Jérôme. He didn't see me. I wanted to take him in my arms, to know more intimately the scent of his power. I alone could love him at that moment, embrace him, kiss his mouth, say to him: "Nicolas, my little brother, my little brother."

For twenty years he had wanted to fight Jérôme. He had finally done it, though even as recently as the night before he had still been ashamed of his lack of resolve.

Once more, Jérôme stood. He was now screaming freely, nonstop. This probably soothed him. He advanced in zigzags, like a drunk. And we followed him. Slowly, patiently, we led him to the room he would never leave again. Afraid this new Jérôme would lose his way, we monitored his final steps.

When we arrived on the plateau, just before the courtyard, we thought he wouldn't reach the gate, that he no longer had the will to cross the few meters that separated him from his bed. He had slightly outpaced us. The wind was blowing up there and cut him off from us. We could no longer hear his moans so clearly. He stopped and began to shake his head violently. Then he raised it to the sky and began to howl, all while trying to stand back up. Automatically, I looked at this sky that he was probably seeing for the last time. It was blue. The sun had come out. It was morning now.

At last, Jérôme set off again. This time I was quite certain he would stop only at his bed. He crossed the gate and we accompanied him to the courtyard in Les Bugues. Tiène and Papa were hitching the cart to go and fetch wood. Jérôme did not see them. They stopped working and watched him until he entered the house.

Papa carefully examined Nicolas, stopped in the middle of the courtyard, then went back to work. Tiène came to ask me what had happened. I told him that Nicolas and Jérôme had fought over Clémence.

"He looks done for," said Tiène. I told him that yes, it did seem quite serious, and that Jérôme might not make it.

Tiène went to fetch Nicolas. He asked him to help hitch Mâ, who can be difficult some summer mornings. Then the men went to the fields.

. . .

Once in bed, Jérôme had the strength to scream again. Maman left work to be at his side. It had been a while since I had thought of Jérôme as Maman's brother. I told Maman that Nicolas had fought with Jérôme because of Clémence, and also because of everything that's been brewing between us for years. I wasn't exaggerating; Jérôme had spent all of our fortune. He is the reason Nicolas and I were never able to study. We never had enough money to leave Les Bugues. Which is also why I'm not yet married. Nicolas married Clémence. She's my adopted sister, but even so she's our maid, and she's ugly and stupid. Two years ago at harvest time, he got her pregnant and was forced to marry her. If Nicolas had known other girls, he wouldn't have been so foolish. He reached that point after years of loneliness. It's not really his fault. He may well not have married Clémence. Maman must remember: it was Jérôme who had pushed him into it. The rest of us didn't agree. Clémence had left for her sister's in Périgueux. It was Jérôme who had gone to fetch her. They were married the following week in Ziès. We had thought it would be easier to get it over with. Did she think we had done the right thing?

I reminded Maman of everything. She forgets easily. I told her I was the one who informed Nicolas that Jérôme had gone up to Clémence's room every night for the last three months. It's true that Nicolas neglected her and that she slept alone. But Clémence had known Nicolas forever, and she should have realized what was in store for her; Clémence should not have gotten married. Wasn't I right?

Maman took my hands in hers, shaking: "And Noël?" I laughed and said: "He's Nicolas's." She asked me how I could be sure. I dragged her to the courtyard and we watched Noël in his playpen.

Noël has straight red hair, violet eyes with fluttering transparent eyelids shimmering all over with red silk. His slippers were off and he was dressed only in a pair of little underpants that were falling down. He turned to stare at Maman. And because she didn't say anything, after a moment he went back to playing his secret game. He struck his playpen with all his might and fell back on his behind each time, without laughing or getting angry. In the sunlight, his little throat was a brownish pink, and it was as if you could see his blood pulsing underneath.

Maman seemed emotional. After a while, she said: "You're right." She went to fetch Noël's hat, stuck it on his head, then returned to Jérôme.

I didn't say anything else to Maman. But Jérôme had to disappear from Les Bugues. So that Nicolas could begin to live. It had to stop someday. That day had come.

. . .

Closer to evening, Jérôme began to howl, and I had to watch the path from the Grand Terrace, to see if anyone was coming up to our house. Les Bugues is beautiful from there. Our meadows are beautiful. Our woods too, which create enormous volumes of shade all around. You can see the horizon clearly from the terrace. Far and wide, in the valley of the Rissole, there are small farms surrounded by fields, woods, and little white hills. I don't know what we would have done if a visitor had come. Nevertheless, I kept a close eye on the path. I thought an idea would probably come to me at the last minute if someone appeared. Deep down, I felt at ease. The sun set and shadows stretched for a long time down the sides of the hills. Near the terrace, there are two magnolia trees. At some point a flower fell on the ledge of the parapet I was leaning on. It smelled like a fallen flower, a scent, almost a flavor, very sweet and already a little rotten. August was here. Clément, at the other end of the path, in the shadow of the hill of Ziès, would soon pen up his sheep for the night. I went back inside. For the last three hours I had been keeping watch. I was sure that no one would venture onto our paths so late.

At Jérôme's door I listened, my ear to the wood. Clémence came to join me. Jérôme was still screaming, begging for the doctor in Ziès. Maman kept answering the same thing in a distracted, dreamy voice, as if to a child asking questions: that the mare was in the fields, and it was unreasonable for us to stop work to go to Ziès. As soon as Maman responded, Jérôme began to harass her again, asking the exact same thing. His jolts of impatience made the bed creak. At times he insulted Maman, but she remained as firm as when she was faced with one of Noël's tantrums, always the same gentleness in her refusal. I felt a desire to insult her too, for her to be slapped because of this refusal. And yet she was doing exactly what had to be done. She did not flinch in the face of Jérôme's supplications. She answered: "No, it's just a bad wound, it's nothing." Jérôme threatened, said that if we didn't call the doctor, he would ride Mâ himself, he would go himself. Then he grew tender: "Tell Françou to go, I beg you; I don't feel well at all, do it for your brother, Anna . . ." Françou, a name he had called me when I was a child. That's how he is, Jérôme, when he needs you. Maman kept responding: "No, Jérôme, no." Maman must have remembered everything I told her that morning.

I entered the bedroom. Clémence disappeared into the hall like a beast that dwells in darkness.

Jérôme was lying down, fully dressed. His lips were blue, his skin jaundiced, an even yellow. Maman, sitting at his side, was reading. The room smelled like iodine, and despite the half-open blinds, it was difficult to imagine the summer raging outside. The sight of Jérôme made me feel cold. I remember wanting to leave. Jérôme was moaning with all his might. His screams rose, muffled at first. It seemed like he was going to vomit himself whole in a thick lava, then from this foam finally emerged the real cry, pure, raw as a child's. Between two moans, the ticking of the clock cleared its path. Jérôme stared at the ceiling light, and the precise heft of his body's flesh was plainly visible. Perhaps I hadn't been entirely sure until then that Jérôme was dying. In strong, regular jolts, his legs and arms stiffened; his mournful cry burst through the rooms, the garden, the courtyard, crossed the field between the path and the forest and crouched in the bushes filled with birds and sunshine. He was a beast we wanted to restrain but that managed to escape the house every time and, once outside, became dangerous to us. Jérôme had not yet lost hope that the outside would rescue him, while knowing that he was alone at Les Bugues with us, who kept him completely out of sight. But we spoke to him gently, and had he looked into our eyes, he would have seen in them a commiseration for his body, which was so big and in so much pain. I remember wanting to leave. But I tried hard to reckon with Jérôme, to get used to his cries, his supplications, so tender at times, his intolerable face. All this, to the point of boredom.

When the men returned, I went to meet them. Nicolas looked exhausted. He said to me: "He's still screaming? If I'd known . . ." It's the only thing my brother said to me during this time, and he could just as easily have said it to anyone. He could have not asked anything at all, since he heard Jérôme screaming. I felt a little anger and a little contempt for Nicolas, and it was irritating in the midst of the joy I now felt in seeing him. If he'd "known," what would he have done? I was curious to know. When I asked him, a bit impatiently, he didn't respond. He left. We saw him lying under the parapet, in the meadow. He seemed angry at us, and at me in particular. He looked unnatural to me. To know we were hanging on his silence, on his slightest gesture, on his first word, which never came but which we waited on, surely troubled him. When he asked me that question, I could see in his eyes that he wasn't thinking of anything specific. Jérôme was not dying fast enough. As for us, what were we doing there spying on him? Above all, Nicolas was sad with that sadness "without reason," like the day after a wedding or the wheat harvest. When the thing is done and no longer has to be done, you look at your hands and feel sadness.

He could be sure with us that nobody would ever know the real reasons behind the fight. So he was not really worried. He just had to remember that Jérôme and

Clémence were sleeping together to justify killing Jérôme. If the reasons for his hatred of Jérôme were vague, this fact was precise. He could recall it constantly, knock his mind against it in moments of doubt. He had the absolute right to do what he had done. But by protecting him from the law, we acted as if we were the ones who gave him this right. We spoiled its purity, and as a result all of Nicolas's pleasure. To please him, we would have had to be reckless.

At some point, Clémence cried out in a muffled voice: "Luce Barragues!" I didn't believe her; I went to the courtyard gate to check. Yes, Luce Barragues was riding her horse up the path to Les Bugues.

I ran to Jérôme's side. His forehead was dripping with sweat. He no longer hoped for anything, he no longer asked for anything, he continued to moan. I dabbed his forehead, I told him to stop complaining: Mâ had returned from the fields, I would go to Ziès and fetch the doctor on the condition that he stop screaming. Jérôme went quiet. From time to time, he opened his mouth. I reminded him of his promise, and he remained silent.

At some point I grazed my finger against his forehead, which was damp and cold. He was dying beneath my hand. He was a thing that could no longer be saved, abandoned.

. . .

Luce took off. The three men sat down at the table for dinner. Clémence served and cleared in silence. Despite Jérôme's screams, the men ate. They looked alike in that moment, deaf to Jérôme's pleas. They were hungry. Nicolas also ate. Over their heads, the lamp swung, and the conjoined shadow of their backs danced against the bare walls. Papa said to me: "You'll go fetch the doctor, Françou." He hadn't believed it was serious that morning, but now he was convinced. There was no mistaking it. He went to see Jérôme and came back dazed. It was at that moment, sitting down at the table, that he told me to go fetch the doctor. The sight of Papa brought back a memory: Ten years ago, when Jérôme came back from Paris after being away for six months. His business affair hadn't worked out and he came back empty-handed, all the money we had left spent. By the next day, he had regained all his confidence and acted as proud, as insolent with Papa as before. And Papa hadn't seemed to notice anything, hadn't said a thing.

And so I went to Ziès. It was night and I could barely see. Four kilometers along the Rissole. Mâ was reluctant to make the trip after her day's work. But she's strong and can't resist the pleasure of trotting along with me on her back. I've been riding her for five years now, we know each other, she and I. It was hot. There was no moon, but after a little while I saw the road, straight and white, very clearly ahead of me. Dry ditches resounded with the chirps of frogs. The little farms in the valley were illuminated, you could count their lights.

Halfway there, I halted Mâ for a moment. She started to graze the grass on the side of the road. Under my dress, hiked up, I felt her moist and muscular sides panting against my bare thighs. What would I say to the doctor? I was certain that at the last minute I would find some explanation, quite naturally. Jérôme was a thing of the past.

I would have liked to linger for a while there, in the darkness. Mâ, sinuous and lopsided, grazed beneath me. Laziness took over me and I fell asleep on her saddle, my head sideways. The countryside was so peaceful. I dreamt of Tiène sitting at the table, calm, handsome. No one had spoken to me during dinner, except Papa when he told me to go fetch the doctor. Neither Tiène nor Nicolas had looked at me. I decided that I would go see Tiène in his bedroom later. Tonight especially, no one would be paying attention. I saw the men of Les Bugues who were waiting for the doctor without admitting it. They needed him to put an end to their wait. It was a wine too strong for them.

Mâ resumed her trot with her light, efficient clip. In the night, in the farms, people must have thought, "That's the Veyrenattes daughter," and fallen back asleep to the sound of Mâ's footsteps, her gait that barely skims the road and dances on the flint while making fiery flowers bloom. That night, soon, Tiène. I clearly remember Mâ's sides against my skin and those thoughts of Tiène at the same time, resembling him: warm.

I didn't pass anyone on the way. I remained lying down atop Mâ, who eased her trot, sensing that I was forgetting she was there.

. . .

The doctor was very young. The old one had died the year before. This one didn't know us yet. He offered to bring me back in his car. I told him I had my horse and that I would go ahead of him. He asked me: "What happened to your uncle? So that I can know what to bring." I told him that Jérôme had been kicked badly by the mare, in the liver. When did it happen? I told him: "This morning." He seemed interested to come to our house. He made small talk. He knew the Veyrenattes, in fact. Les Bugues, too. It's very beautiful from the road, the two gables of the old house. He talked to me in the consultation area next to the dining room where I had entered and his voice resounded, clear. He was finishing dinner when I arrived; there was an open book on the table, which hadn't yet been cleared. The room had been refurbished, it was clean and white. In the next room, the kitchen, I could hear the maid cleaning up. Suddenly, as he was preparing his bag, I felt just how tired I was. I let myself fall onto a chair along the wall, my head leaning on the dresser. That's when I was struck out of nowhere by a certitude that what was happening to us was not important.

We had been waiting for it for so long; I dreamt of it at night. I dreamt that it had happened, the thing that would set us free. It's impossible that the others hadn't dreamt of it too. Since this morning, I had believed it. I believed that it had happened. I was feeling good. And suddenly, it seemed to me once again that I had been dreaming of it all along. What did it mean, Jérôme's death? Jérôme, who was screaming up there. If this was our first step into freedom, it wasn't much.

I closed my eyes from sudden weariness. The doctor appeared in front of me. "Are you all right, Mademoiselle Veyrenattes?" He had metal-rimmed glasses, pimples around his mouth, slicked-back shiny blond hair. I said that Jérôme wasn't well at all, that he was a goner. He thought for a minute and he asked me a few questions about Mâ's kick. Then he went to grab the morphine. "The worry here is a ruptured kidney. Does your uncle drink?" His tone had changed; he was indifferent. I said that he drank, I added that he must have known it, that around here people knew, everyone, all those . . .

We left. I took off at a gallop. I had told him to wait for me when he reached Les Bugues; he wouldn't find the path at the intersection, there were ten paths that went into the woods. Really, I didn't want him to beat me to Jérôme's bedroom in case Jérôme talked about his quarrel.

Jérôme wouldn't have bragged about it, I knew, but I had my concerns anyway.

Mâ was not happy. She approached the car frothing. The doctor waited for me. I let the mare go back on her own and we drove on together. When we reached the plateau, we could hear Jérôme. I felt as though I had abandoned a child; I no longer recognized his voice. His pleas had intensified. They were no longer shouted, but rasped, scraped from the bottom of the stomach, stripped of their last modesty, raw; it was as if you could hear the air rustling on the plateau as his screams traversed it. It embarrassed us. The doctor stopped short. He gripped my arm and we listened. It was pitch-black, but I saw his round metallic glasses gleaming. He said to me abruptly: "He's dying! Those are death rattles. Why didn't you call for me earlier?" I asked him not to frighten Jérôme, who was very impressionable. Now we had to avoid the worst. Jérôme would only say something in the grip of terror.

In the dining room, only Tiène was waiting for us. He stood up. He put his hands in his pockets and went out without greeting the doctor. I could tell that he was exasperated. I had left him there, amidst these screams. When he went out, I felt as though he was abandoning me.

Papa and Maman were standing in Jérôme's bedroom. They were giving him compresses and dabbing his forehead. The doctor greeted them, then started to examine Jérôme. His face had taken on a bizarre greenish-yellow color. You could no longer distinguish his lips from the rest of his face. They were puffed up like his eyelids. His pillow was drenched with sweat. His teeth were chattering. The doctor asked me again: "How long ago?" I told him the truth: "This morning." Jérôme watched the man. "I'm suffering, Doctor, it's excruciating, here." He pointed to his side. The doctor lifted his shirt. It was dark blue and very swollen around his liver. When the doctor touched him, Jérôme yelped even louder. He lowered the shirt. Slowly, he took a vial out of his bag and injected Jérôme. Five minutes went by during which Jérôme and the doctor stared at each other. My parents left. The doctor smiled and played with my uncle's wrist. On his face, satisfaction and certitude. Jérôme started to bat his eyelids, then his screams became spaced out by intervals of silence during which he licked his lips. His screams gradually came back to the surface of the living. The doctor whispered to me: "It's morphine." Jérôme groaned more and more softly, then almost deliciously, his screams stretched out into the night. Finally, they ceased. He fell asleep. I pulled the covers over him. We left him and went into the dining room. The doctor turned to me: "Can I speak to you? Yes? Your parents? It's okay with them? Your uncle is beyond saving, you can still take him to Périgueux, but it's no use." We spoke for a moment. I was tired. It was useless to talk. I didn't know what to do with this doctor. He was shocked that no one was around. I, too, thought that Papa and Maman should have been there. I told him that they were old and tired. He gave me several vials of morphine and a syringe and showed me how to administer it. There was nothing else to be done? Nothing. I thanked him. He left.

I closed the doors of the house. I turned off the lights. No one appeared. Before going upstairs, I passed my parents' bedroom. They were already asleep in their big bed planted right in the center of the room. They were sleeping with their backs to each other. I stayed near them for a moment as they slept. Maman had had me in her forties. Papa was almost fifty. Old parents. Maman's hair always smells like vanilla. Papa sleeps the way he lives. His sleep is as discreet and elusive as that of an insect. The window was open onto the pitch-black courtyard. It was very late.

. . .

In the night, Jérôme started to scream again.

Every night until his death, when the evening injection I gave him wore off, he would start to suffer again, to scream. He would wake everyone up, but no one dared complain. No one got up, except me. I would go down, I would find him each time ice cold, drenched in sweat. Awake in the darkness, afraid to die. In those moments, between two death rattles, the sweetest names came out of his mouth. He told me I was his little Françou, the only person who had ever understood him. I would give him an injection and wait by his side for a moment.

Sometimes, when the injection started to take effect, he would smile timidly at me, so that I would smile back, so that he would no longer be afraid. He ate nothing and lost weight. I think that in those last days, he no longer had the strength to feel even suffering. It was terror that made him scream. I would go down to be near him, so that he wouldn't be alone.

One night, falling asleep, he sought my hand and asked me to fetch the notary. I said: "Why the notary?" He didn't have a penny to his name. He didn't insist. The next day, he started asking again for me to fetch the notary, knowing it was useless. He probably liked for me to hear him repeat it. He could still harbor a vague hope that I found it useless because he was not going to die.

We fetched the doctor again. People believed Jérôme had been kicked by Mâ; they came to see how he was doing.

The days passed, each the same as the last. But Jérôme's death couldn't be far off. We could feel it growing more imminent with each day. We had been waiting for a long time. I remember that obstinacy, that tactfulness we deployed, never speaking about it. As if each of us was wary of the others. And yet we were more united than ever.

The men brought in the wheat. Then they chopped down the wood in the forest. We had to start preparing for winter. It was already the end of August.

I never went up to Tiène's room and he never came to find me. Nicolas spoke only to Tiène and Clémence. We saw him at meals; the rest of the time, he worked as usual. We were no more exasperated than in the first days. This reprieve prolonged his act. It allowed him to come to terms with it, to approve of it. Perhaps if Jérôme had died right away, the brutality of it all would have rendered him more prone to remorse. But now he could let himself imagine that Jérôme was not dying. He must have felt such intense regret that he forced himself to believe that if he hadn't killed Jérôme, Jérôme would still have needed to be killed.

It had been exactly nine days since the fight. Jérôme died during the night of the tenth day. He hadn't called for me during the night. When I woke and saw the early morning through my bedroom windows, I understood that he must be dead. I fetched Tiène and we went down together. Jérôme was dead. His mouth was open and his hands dangling, forgotten, on either side of him, slender. He had stopped sweating. His face was no longer swollen as when he had been screaming. His head lay heavy atop his neck. The bed was in a motionless disorder, frozen in the state of Jérôme's final movements. The room now exuded a great calm. That death seemed to me as far from my own death as that of Tiène, as from death itself as we always imagine it. It must have happened early in the night and now Jérôme was no longer terrifying, he was dead, which is to say eternally under the shelter of death. Jérôme had succeeded in leaving us, in hoisting himself there all alone, by his own strength. He hadn't called out; I would never know whether he died stupidly, in his sleep, or whether he had woken up first and refused to call for me. But because of the disdain I suspected he had for us in the end, I completely ceased, then and there, to hold anything against him.

We arranged his sheets and brought his arms along his body in the middle of the bed. With Tiène's help, I closed his mouth with a handkerchief that I knotted around his head. He was heavy, his head especially, now like his feet and knees, nothing but dead weight.

I opened the curtains. Tiène told me it wasn't worth it. But he let me do it. His silence, I noticed, was different from normal. He didn't really have anything to say to me. He approached me at the window. It was barely dawn. No one was up yet. Tiène looked with me at the overgrown garden where we never went, at the blue haze resting between the trees. In front of us, along the pathway, little red roses born in the night were waiting for the sun. We could already hear a few birds. We didn't think to call the others. I saw Tiène's face so close to mine. A smear of white day illuminated it. I stared at him from up close as he stared into the distance. His mouth was relaxed, nearly open. Between his lips, his breath passed and passed again; I watched it lightly fog up the air. His hair smelled like dawn, as though he had slept outside.

I brought him to the kitchen to pour him a cup of coffee. No one had woken up yet. No sound. We felt extremely alone all of a sudden. Brusquely he placed his hand on my hip and pressed me against him. He did this at that moment, only to then leave me for many days without so much as a word to me. He asked if I was cold. For a few seconds, I thought of nothing. Strange things passed before my eyes. The little town of R. in Belgium, silent cities, deserted squares, the sea. We drank our coffee in silence.

Noël cried. We heard walking in the house. I said to Tiène that perhaps we could go to Ziès to fetch the doctor for the official report and all the funeral formalities. "That's true," he replied. "I hadn't thought of that." Clémence appeared with Noël in her arms, Noël was smiling. Clémence had just gotten out of bed; her straight hair hung over her shoulders. As she did every morning, she asked me: "So?" I said that Jérôme was dead. She set Noël on a chair and left again abruptly. Noël was still smiling; he started to play with the fringe of the tablecloth.

. . .

Papa and Maman were in the living room seated side by side. They barely acknowledged the condolences. They were always trying to speak about something else. At the end of the day, Maman said: "So and so still hasn't come, and this person and that person." And then the next morning, she sat back down with Papa in the living room to receive the neighbors.

We rarely used the living room. It always reminded me of the little town of R. in Belgium where Papa had been burgomaster. On this same armchair with the black oak arms, after that infamous reception nineteen years ago, Papa had sat me on his knees and said, caressing my hair: "We're going to leave for France, my little Françou."

Apart from the town civil servants, no one had come to Maman's reception.

In a corner of the large living room, a three-violin orchestra was playing the polka. Papa had opened the ball with the wife of the senior city councilman. No one had followed his lead, and for a quarter of an hour Papa had danced alone with her. I can still see that woman's face. In Papa's arms, she let herself get a bit drunk off disgust. The civil servants had left right after the first dance, after dipping their lips into the champagne coupes. On their way out, they surrounded the wife of the city councilman who had danced with Papa and who now wore a heroic mask. The orchestra had shared the lunch. We remained alone in the large living room, the four of us. I don't know what happened then, because we fell asleep, Nicolas and I, on armchairs. In the morning we found Papa and Maman in the same position as the night before. They were talking in lowered voices, heads still, and if not for the few words that came out of their mouths, we would have thought they were asleep, eyes open, in their party clothes. From time to time one of them would offer a remark about the previous night's party in a soft voice. Their words held no bitterness against the civil servants. Maman said: "It's impossible, impossible . . ." and Papa replied: "It's true." Maman continued: "And I didn't count the earrings of Aunt Nano." And Papa: "It's much more than anyone thought." I remember that at a certain point he said: "I don't want them to see you in the city. You'll take the night train."

I half closed my eyes, I didn't dare reveal to them that I was awake. The electric lamps had remained illuminated in the autumn morning that was already peeking through the windows. No maid appeared and the whole house was still silent. Behind the foliage, we could see the musicians' chairs and the lunch table, uncleared, shining, ravaged with light. Father said: "You'll tell Jérôme to accompany you."

I knew that the month before, Jérôme had dragged Papa into his stock exchange business and that Papa, obliged to pay for Jérôme's debts, had taken the money from the city hall's charity box. It was known in the town. Papa hadn't had time to replace the money before the region prefect's inspection. "They can't say he's guilty," Maman said, referring to Jérôme. Papa answered that no, he was not, since he, the burgomaster, had been the one to take the money to give to him. Jérôme couldn't have done it, he wouldn't have done it. It was Jérôme who had asked him to do it. But he had been in a panic. And all he'd had to do was refuse. "He'll help you with the move," Papa said. "I'll go to Anvers tomorrow. For now Nano's earrings will suffice," said Maman.

It was ten years ago that Papa had been burgomaster in R. But what were those ten years compared to the future looming ahead of them, for which no measure had yet been invented? I was still very little. But I saw very quickly, perhaps as soon as that morning, that they drew no vanity from their misfortune. They accepted it until they no longer suffered from it. They sought simply to heal, to repair things.

In the end, I revealed that I was awake. I went to Papa. I stopped in front of him. He stared at me for a long time without moving. Maman also did not speak or move even a finger. The sun had risen and was playing with the dust on the rug. Papa looked at me with curiosity. His eyes moved from my face to my bare calves to my flat chest sealed inside my ballgown. Over the course of a single night, he had become a deposed burgomaster, worse than dishonored, who would no longer make speeches in city hall, who would no longer wear the scarf of his town, who would no longer be greeted in the streets. A man with no choice but to go elsewhere. That little girl was still with him as his arms were, with years to live. But his duties as burgomaster had no doubt kept him from really seeing her until then, and he must have remembered her suddenly. At that moment Papa's hands released the armchair they'd been gripping since the night before, and he sat me on his knees.

That was nineteen years ago. Since then, we haven't budged from Les Bugues. Now I'm almost twenty-six years old. The days have seemed long to me since Jérôme's death, and I've thought again of my youth and of that scene several times because I had nothing to do but watch people slowly ascend toward the trees to give their condolences. Papa and Maman stayed in the living room side by side, silent. People could barely see them when they arrived from outside, so thick was the darkness. They spoke little, and people must have deemed their silence appropriate. People left the living room, seemingly lost; they rapidly shook my hand on their way out and left.

. . .

The second day, some men came to Ziès to bring Jérôme's coffin. It was about four o'clock. There hadn't been any visitors. They had to call everyone to place him in the coffin. But there was only Papa, Maman, and me in Les Bugues. Tiène and Nicolas had left. Not to work, but to get some air, they had said. Clémence, in her bedroom, was probably crying. For thirteen days she had been crying nonstop, waiting for someone to remember her.

We had directed the coffin bearers to Jérôme's bedroom. It was hot in there because of the closed shutters. The coffin smelled like polished wood. It was flared at the shoulders and narrowed to a point at the feet. The men found my uncle and lifted him into the coffin. He was completely straight, seemingly stiff. One of the men placed a small saucer of holy water and a boxwood branch on the nightstand. All that was left to do was close the coffin. The man assumed a solemn air and said: "The family? To bless him." Then they waited for us to bless Jérôme; one by one. Papa and Maman seemed embarrassed; they didn't know what to do. They hunched their shoulders and seemed old and childish. They hadn't considered it. I sensed that they were unable to bless Jérôme. And they also couldn't make up their minds not to do it. They were ashamed not to be able to decide in front of these men. But their shame would have been even greater had they agreed to do it. Later, I thought again of their hesitation. They certainly could have taken the branch and made the sign of the cross over Jérôme, as they had received our neighbors and accepted their condolences. However, their hands remained clasped. The two men could have waited till night, and still my parents would not have performed the gesture. Perhaps they were hypocritical. But no one could have forced them to pronounce words of regret. They could have told themselves that they hadn't lied to anyone, in the sense that Jérôme's death had forced us into a certain attitude in front of strangers. They probably did tell themselves that, so they could be at peace with themselves. To bless our uncle would have been to overly conceal the indifference with which they had watched him die. It would mean, at the age of sixty, to consent to lying, even the most natural lie. If they had done it, they surely would not have been able to live afterward with the same ease. They knew it. That is what froze them in place. Me too. I knew they wouldn't do it, that sign that had to be made, based on a religion that they had done without for so long that it held no more meaning.

In the end, I told the men that they could do what they had to do. Then they closed the coffin and sealed the lid. The bedroom smelled like varnished oak. We heard the little squeals of copper screws in the smooth wood. The men didn't have any trouble and they worked with care.

Then they placed the closed coffin on the tall stools they had brought with them.

I didn't realize what we had just done. The men said: "Okay, all done." They lifted their caps and left. We listened to their truck drive into the distance. I understood that I would never see Jérôme again. I remember that once the men had left, we stayed planted there, the three of us, embarrassed over the same thing. We had not looked at Jérôme one last time. I suddenly found it revolting that we would be cut off from him forever without having been alerted more formally that they were about to seal him up. They had surprised us. I said to myself that if I had seen him again one last time, I would have learned something definitive about what Jérôme had meant to us. I had in my ears the grinding of screws, more and more unpleasant to my memory; I couldn't manage to leave. Then, in the end, I said to myself that if I had seen him, I would have wanted to see him still another last time, and so there could not in fact be a last time. I made up my mind and left. It's the only regret I have about Jérôme, that I didn't look at him expressly before never seeing him again. But I could have had this regret about anyone, about any death.

Some elderly women came to say prayers around the wooden box for two nights. They didn't speak to anyone. Elderly women who left at day break after having a cup of coffee that we poured for them, Clémence and I. Disinterested, they kept vigil for all the dead of the plain of the Rissole. They came in twos, in threes, always different women, for each wanted her turn. In the morning they would leave again, skeletal, so light in their black skirts.

. . .

The night before the burial, around four in the morning, Clémence came into my bedroom and woke me. She was fully dressed. She held a suitcase in one hand and Noël in the other. She called me sweetly by my name: "You understand, Francine, that I can't stay here anymore. I'm going to stay with my sister, the one in Périgueux." I asked her what she planned to do with Noël. She told me that was the terrible part, but she didn't know. Fat tears fell from her eyes onto her blouse. She had agonized over it so much that she had lost her head. If she had thought she was to blame, the punishment she was waiting for hadn't come. She had figured out that she could continue to live in Les Bugues as long as she didn't expect a single kind gesture from us, as long as she lived alone with her child. She preferred to flee.

I had never imagined how much Jérôme and Clémence had cared for each other. They had loved each other in the darkness of the attic, they had hid themselves away from us. Clémence must have had a sweet stomach, soft and milky breasts, a limp strength that was easily deflated. Jérôme, in his old age, must have found her generous. I had undone that thing between them that was pretty dismal, but that had allowed them to tolerate existence in Les Bugues. I asked myself why. Perhaps to no longer know they were hiding up there. Of course, I hadn't wanted Nicolas to kill Jérôme, just for Jérôme to be chased away. But now I didn't know what I had wanted exactly. I was tired. Why had I denounced them? One day I would know, I was sure of it. For now I was tired, I had no desire to reflect.

I didn't stop Clémence from leaving. I gave her a bit of money and told her to leave Noël; Nicolas was in a bad way, and he should have his son with him. Clémence looked at me without seeming to understand. Then her face suddenly widened like a rock hitting water. Brusquely, she handed me Noël and took off running. I heard her rush down the stairs with rapid little steps, cross the courtyard, and that was that. I had taken Jérôme from her,

I had not held her back for Nicolas's sake, and yet she had given me her son, just like that, without even trying to convince me that she should keep him. I imagined her running the four kilometers to Ziès at night, all alone. But I couldn't think of it for long. It wasn't worth forcing myself to pity her; I had never managed it, I wouldn't manage it tonight. In the same vein, I would never be angry with her, even after what she did. And everyone here was like me. The best thing, in fact, was to let her leave for her sister's.

I held Noël in my arms for a moment: the child of Clémence and Nicolas. I didn't know what to do with him, where to set him down until morning. I was tired, I wanted to take Nicolas's son to him, but I knew that, annoyed at being awoken in the middle of the night, he would reproach me for letting Clémence leave. The next day, however, he would approve of what I had done; he would feel liberated. For now, I had to look after Noël. He screamed, he cried. It was only four in the morning. What to do, oh what to do? I placed him on my bed, I leaned my head against the wall so as not to see him anymore, I blocked my ears so as not to hear him anymore. Life was really nothing but chaos, and anger overtook me.

Chaos, boredom, chaos. It began one night during the harvest when Nicolas impregnated her. And gradually, chaos led to more chaos, and everyone had let it happen. Of course they were afraid, already bothered by the idea of any kind of change, Nicolas, my parents, everyone. Suddenly I noticed my anger, noticed that chaos lived in me too. It surged through my body; the boredom surrounding me was black, a never-ending night. I thought of my age, the age of all those sleeping in this house, and I heard time gnaw at us like an army of rats. We were good seeds. We had let him live for twenty-four years. We had counted on time to impose order on the affairs of the house. Time had passed. Chaos had won out even so. It was now a chaos of souls, of blood. We could no longer heal, we no longer wanted to. We no longer knew how to want to be free, we were dreamers, degenerates, people who dream of happiness, a true happiness that will overwhelm it all. With Jérôme dead, Clémence remained. And our nonchalance, twenty-four years old. We still pleased ourselves, and we desired nothing else in the end except to continue to believe that we were made for an impossible life.

The others were sleeping. As usual, of course. Each in their own bed sleeping their own sleep. I stayed up. Always the same thing. I had Noël, Noël born of chaos and boredom. When I think about it now that it's all over, I remember that soon I was no longer angry at anyone except myself, mainly because those ideas had come to me and I hadn't been able to chase them away.

I decided to take Noël up to Tiène. This little one had been passed around and around, this little one that I had just realized was the living progeny of chaos and boredom. I took him up to Tiène; he screamed in my arms, hardened by anger, formidable. Tiène must have been awakened by his cries. Sprawled, his hands under his head, he was smoking. "What's going on?"

I told him that Clémence had left and that I had told her to leave the little one. I asked him what we were going to do with him. As I spoke, I saw Tiène half sitting up in his bed, the form of his body. Why is he so beautiful that you can't help but stare at him, even amid so much anger? Why is he so desirable, so disconcerting, so full of silence that any word uttered in his presence is a lie? He smiled at me, his face aged and rejuvenated endlessly, and inside me day turned to darkness, cool to hot.

How could Tiène love me? I felt a hundred years older. I was born in a miserable time and I don't have the strength and I would never think to hope for anything for myself alone. One day, he showed up here and stayed. He gave me only false reasons for coming here, I know. Why did Tiène leave an excellent family for one so dull? How could Tiène desire me, Tiène whose face I inhale like a forest fresh with morning? I, who am ugly, why would he want to make me smile?

He said Noël must be hungry because he had been woken up in the middle of the night. He put on his jacket. He told me to go to bed. He would go down with Noël to the kitchen and give him some milk to drink. Then he would keep him in his bed until tomorrow.

I left them and went back to bed. I couldn't fall back asleep. My body was numb. It felt nice and calm, hanging from my head, utterly resolved to be deaf, not to listen to me. But my head took flight freely in a waking delirium.

The sky turned white over the fir trees in the garden, and the bells tolled. There are moments when I forget Tiène, when I can no longer remember him at all. He becomes of such insignificance that I can no longer recall either his features or his voice. Even though he's so close to me, up there in a bedroom on the second floor.

Here's the dawn; the night cracks all over. You thought it would be eternal. You should have slept. Because here's another, an immense day that will last until tonight. Everything has already passed. Everything has already passed to the other side, even Jérôme's death, tipped into the abyss where the days pile up once they've been emptied, even my life that drags alongside the years and my age without ever falling in.

It's the morning of the burial. When will the world stop? When will people stop burying their dead with such care? When after dawn will I no longer love Tiène?

. . .

Lots of people came to the burial. Some who barely knew us. We had never seen so many people in Les Bugues.

The coffin was brought out and placed on a black truck that was for Jérôme alone. There were two other trucks for the living. They all went, Tiène and Nicolas too.

I remained alone in Les Bugues with Noël, whom someone had to watch. It was nice out. Noël was still asleep. I milked our two cows, took out Mâ, fed the hens and the rabbits. At the top of Ziès, Clément watched over the sheep; his dog yipped and ran across the hill. I thought about how it was almost time to shear the sheep, almost time to harvest the potatoes, to trim the tobacco, to shell the beans, in the evening, on the large granary table. The wheat had been brought in, we had to go sell it in Périgueux. We had lost time over the last two weeks, we had to catch up. With Clémence gone, we might need someone to replace her. With two fewer people at the table, we might manage.

I went back to the house. The air smelled like flowers, the tables had been pushed against the walls, the doors were open. I went into Jérôme's bedroom; I locked the door and put the key in the pocket of my apron. Then I went to fetch Noël from Tiène's bedroom; he was awake, babbling about inarticulate benign things. The sun filled the room and reflected off his wet, translucent mouth, and his cheeks danced with pink shadows. In his pupils, light gleamed and revealed green and violet crystals like the ones in the shallows of the Rissole on summer days.

I had to change him, feed him his porridge. Last night, I had been irritated with him. He reached out his arms to me and I held him. On my face, I felt the warmth of his cheek and his light breath. It smelled like hot hay. This one is called Noël Veyrenattes, he hatched and assumed his place twenty months ago in the stomach of a woman, a very poor woman. I don't really know what I felt. I squeezed Noël tightly in my arms, holding myself back from squeezing any harder. I wanted to make it up to him by melting his fresh feebleness into my already old strength.

I dressed him and fed him lunch. Then I arranged the chairs and tables, gave the house a sense of calm and order. It was already noon when I went out with Noël. They wouldn't be back for another three hours at least. They would eat in Ziès, then they'd come back on foot; it would take at least three hours.

With Jérôme's key in my pocket—the final period of a book—I went to the well. I lifted the top and threw in the key. I couldn't risk Maman or Nicolas rifling through Jérôme's things tonight. It was as though the key descended into my body, frozen and hard. I heard the noise it made when it reached the bottom. Jérôme, that beautiful bare-chested man, would not appear anymore at the door of the house. Jérôme: he had simply been that arrogance seated at the table next to us that would leave no trace. It was over.

I went with Noël into the little clearing in the forest behind the barn, and we waited for the others to return.

Noël fell asleep in the crook of my arm. At one point, he was hungry and searched with his hand for my breast. He smiled in his sleep. He woke up, and we laughed together. Then he fell asleep again and began to suckle the breast I had taken out of my dress. In his sleep, his mouth slipped and hung open, wet. The suction sound he made while suckling, so slight, revealed to me that I had a body that was still very young despite my thick and ancient fatigue. I felt it coursing with a series of shivers so new, so morning-like, that I laughed to myself.

We were at ease, the two of us. We saw the blue sky above us, and at our feet, sprawled on the sides of the hills, our forests, dense and somber. At a certain point, I saw that Clément was bringing in his sheep. His dog yipped and the animals left in a soft and sluggish sound of prairie rustling. I don't know if I fell asleep right away. I dreamed of a gentle landscape that reminded me of Les Bugues, a place it seemed I had left a long time ago.

When I opened my eyes again, people were coming up the road. They were walking in single file, curiously; sometimes they clumped and sometimes they separated. In the approaching night, their group formed a smear of moving, amorphous shadow.

. . .

They came back from Ziès with Luce Barragues. Nicolas had heard from me that Clémence had left; he had told Luce, and that must be why she had come to Les Bugues.

In the two years since Nicolas's marriage, she hadn't returned to the house. She would pass by from time to time, but she wouldn't dismount her horse and would leave after a while. Just enough time to show herself to

Nicolas, and then she'd take off. Nicolas had never tried to hold her back. As she receded into the distance, he would lean on the terrace balustrade and watch her go. Sometimes she would turn around: they would stare at each other from a distance for a few seconds and then she would whip her horse. Nicolas would come back from the terrace pale, exhausted with impatience. He would then go search for Clémence in every room of the house. When that happened, Clémence would hide. He would drive her out of the dark vestibule and bring her into the light of the dining room. He would say nothing to her, and even so she would tremble. There before her, Nicolas would live out the moment when, one night, he would hold Luce back by force in front of everyone. Then he would collapse onto an armchair and close his eyes, his head bowed over his chest. Clémence was standing before him, her arms dangling. She watched him lift his face with his eyes shining, his features tense. His wet lips were swollen; Luce's lips came to mind. Clémence started to cry and asked what he wanted. At first he said he didn't want anything, then he asked her how Noël was doing or how she was settling into the house. He seemed to forget that they had been married for a year. In those moments, he must have felt for her a kind of tender surprise. He had to concede that aside from him, she was enduring life in Les Bugues, that she was still there. This gave her a sense of real existence, which was surprising and curious to him. But Clémence saved herself. Taking refuge in her kitchen, alone, she would insult him in whispers through her sobs.

For two years, Luce remained unapproachable, terribly exact in her absence. She had always shown up just often enough to keep Nicolas from forgetting her.

. . .

I never knew what they had said to each other that caused Luce to come back the very evening of Jérôme's burial, the day after Clémence's departure.

Nicolas had probably confided in her that Jérôme had never been kicked by Mâ, and that he was the one who had struck him. But I don't know for certain.

She leapt over, right away, shameless. She came on such a fiery impulse that she drove shame, barely born, underground, ashamed of itself. She wanted Nicolas without delay, still fresh from Jérôme's murder, still clumsy from the freedom of Clémence's departure.

Everyone was hungry, and we started dinner while it was still light out. Nicolas supplemented the ceiling light with an old floor lamp we hadn't used since Belgium. In Luce's honor.

We slaughtered two nice hens. A golden, joyous odor hung in the air. We had that hunger you get after days outside; we felt the need to flee the hazy horizon of fields where the eye can never find its focus, to feel surrounded by four walls within reach. "It'll be ready soon," said Luce Barragues, "be patient, boys." And she laughed. She removed her black coat to reveal a summer dress. Not very tall, slim with round, soft, sun-kissed shoulders. Black hair that caressed her neck and swished, swished endlessly, blue eyes, a very beautiful and very precise face that continually came undone in a silent laugh. We thought we knew her. Her mother dead, she lived alone with the Barragues father and two younger brothers. She was rich, with maids. Hands hardened only by the mare's reins. Sometimes, on summer mornings, I would cross paths with her near Ziès, and we would race our horses. I remembered a white face and lips mauve with the cold of morning under her blue eyes. But I had never seen her laugh in the light, arms bare, throat bare, between two men. She walked through the room as though still on her horse. Her gentlest gestures created wind, unleashed an aroma of wind. She was everywhere around us. We were stunned, dumbfounded. It was the night of the burial and we no longer knew what the real course of things was. Each of us felt that we had reached the end of our old slowness; we were verging on impatience, on exuberance perhaps.

At the table, she showed us how to laugh. At ease, while eating, she would laugh in Nicolas's face. He was forcing himself to be serious, and yet we sensed that he could have laughed at anything at the slightest pretext. He wasn't the same brother anymore. I made him slightly uncomfortable. He no longer knew what to look at, what to say, how to use his hands to eat and drink. A dangerous joy choked him; sometimes it spurted from him in a word, a laugh, a gesture that he couldn't hold back. It seemed as though he might die of it. He tried to throw himself once and for all into a flood of natural laughter in which the importance and pride choking him since the Jérôme affair would be swept away. He looked all over, he even turned around, and his hands shook from the same search as his eyes. Luce was opposite him. He was still searching for her. He couldn't believe it. He didn't see her. He wished he could still tell her that he had been the one to kill Jérôme. From time to time, his gaze rushed back toward her. Then he would look again to the courtyard, search for her again. He tried to glimpse her between the trees, on her horse.

The meal continued. Sometimes, while speaking, she would take Nicolas's hand in her own, but he wouldn't let her and sharply withdrew. Luce laughed even harder. She said she had known for a long time that Nicolas was weird, but not so weird that he kept himself from being joyful when he wanted to be. She shouldn't have said that. She was afraid that Nicolas would not pull himself together again, but he didn't pay attention. The others didn't seem to notice anything either. Everyone was listening to Luce with a mixture of fervor and distraction, as to a piece of music.

For years now Luce and Nicolas had wanted to know the taste of each other's mouths. Since Nicolas's wedding, there had existed between them an old mute quarrel that had never dissipated. And Nicolas was a bit brusque with Luce because he didn't want to resolve that quarrel just yet. He didn't want to be happy so fast, he didn't understand that he was already happy. He would have felt remorse at leaving his old sadness behind so soon.

When Luce said that he was weird, for some reason I felt like he was my little brother again. "Weird." Nicolas danced in my head above that word, aged with all the ages that he had been in succession; he spun around it, escaped it, returned to it endlessly, sometimes as small as Noël, sometimes sweating and trembling from his fight with Jérôme. I saw him there that night standing on the wave of that vague word, slender, dreamy, like a dancer. From one minute to the next, he would succumb to happiness. I wished he would remember me, look at me. Simply take my hand and kiss it, remind himself for example that I had been there when he killed Jérôme. I wished we could speak one last time of that morning as of a thing born of our love, for the two of us alone. But he avoided my gaze. Of that, he would speak from now on only to Luce. And that's why, in the distance, beyond my joy, I felt like a sad corpse, brotherless.

We spoke mainly of Nicolas. Of Nicolas before his marriage, of his childhood, and I was mixed into the stories we made of it. Luce reminded us of our time on the banks of the Rissole during the first summers we spent in Les Bugues.

Tiène got up often to fetch more bottles of wine. Everyone was thirsty. It was probably because Tiène was a bit tipsy that he also seemed to remember how Luce and I had nearly suffocated Nicolas teaching him to whistle into a blade of elderberry, and our terror, and our subsequent doggedness in continuing this terrible game despite our fear.

Papa and Maman flanked me at the table. They spoke little. They listened to us; they answered the questions they were asked. They had hardly any memories of our childhood in Les Bugues because they were working a lot at the time and hadn't taken much care of us. I remember the Nicolas stories better than they do, I remember our past better than anyone. That's why I talked so much. Tiène mixed into our conversation. He laughed with us. We almost forgot that he hadn't grown up in Les Bugues. He was probably laughing at his own memories. But he said nothing about them, out of discretion, so that everything that night was about my brother.

As we spoke, I noticed Nicolas was listening to me avidly while feigning a superior indifference. He was sitting next to Luce. Through his open shirt, I saw his smooth chest, golden in the light. His arms no longer withdrew as sharply when they touched Luce's arms. Watching them, you couldn't help but think of their naked bodies. Next to Luce's black hair, Nicolas's hair seemed a light chestnut, striped with near-blond streaks, lightened by the sun. They had likely drunk too much wine. At the end of the meal, their heads sometimes drew near and touched. They looked like two young animals playing. When they laughed, their lips and teeth gleamed under their laughter, like sunny things.

Nicolas spoke sometimes but only to mention that Luce had played with us, that she had been there on such and such an occasion.

From time to time, I looked outside. The forest was already completely blue. It must have been late. Underneath the parapet was the line of triangular peaks of the black firs.

At a certain point, Clément walked across the courtyard to return to his home on the hill of Ziès. He was carrying a bucket of sheep's milk. As he passed, he looked at our table, all illuminated amid the six of us, joyful. He turned his head away, saluted us with his hat, and left. Apart from me, no one had seen him pass. I didn't dare look outside for too long for fear of revealing that I didn't actually find myself near them but over there, with Clément, on the already dark paths that I remembered like distant places. It was the first time we had recalled the past like this as a family. Speaking about it for so long to Luce, for Luce, I felt it sprawl in my memory, desolate. For the two of them, on the other hand, the same past came into the light of day, all in bloom. Even in our memories, Nicolas had forgotten me. I wanted to be alone, to stop talking with them, so I could think freely.

At the end of the meal, I saw that Tiène was distracted. He was looking at the courtyard too. He said that it must be late and that never before tonight had he felt so profoundly how removed Les Bugues felt from it all.

Papa and Maman seemed tired. They were no longer listening. Papa was dozing off. He told us, smiling, that he was getting old and that he was no longer young enough to stay up late.

We rose from the table.

Nicolas, Tiène, and Luce went into the workshop. I stayed alone with Maman. She complimented me and told me that I had done a nice job tidying the house. She asked me whether I had taken care of Jérôme's room. I put her at ease: the bedroom was tidied; there was nothing in there that we needed to worry about, we would open it up later on, for the winter cleaning. I had the key. We'd see to it later. Maman did not insist. She looked tired, but she didn't seem to want to go to bed.

"Sit down with me, just for a minute."

We sat down next to each other along the wall of the dining room.

"You haven't said anything to me in two weeks, Françou. We haven't had time to talk. Where is Clémence?"

I told her briefly about Clémence's departure. I had been taking care of Noël. Right now he was asleep upstairs. I'd fed him before dinner. She didn't need to worry about the future. I would always take care of Noël. It was for the best that Clémence had gone back to Périgueux.

"And Nicolas? What will Nicolas do? And you, Françou? Our lives are about to change."

She spoke rapidly. Suddenly she remembered that I wasn't married. I knew that this was Maman's most persistent worry, but she never spoke of it directly to anyone. She would no doubt view Jérôme's death as the herald of an era of all kinds of change to our existence. Jérôme was dead, so nothing was totally impossible; I might even manage to get married.

She placed her hands in mine and almost as quickly, she forgot what she had just said, as usual. I gripped her hands very firmly and she was gradually reassured.

She had grown thinner and older that night; in her black taffeta dress, it was more visible than other days. I felt her fingers between mine, hard and gnarled like roots. Her feet poked out from under her skirt, bound in tiny polished boots.

I asked her whether she was sad because of Jérôme's death. She told me yes, of course. I noticed suddenly that she was old. But it was true that she had always seemed old to me, the oldest of all the women. I think it was the memory of the city of R. in Belgium that had rendered her indifferent to everything around her for the last twenty years. She had started to think about it after she left, to think again endlessly of her youth, which had passed by without her noticing. Often, at night, I knew that they spoke about it together, she and Papa, sometimes for a long while. Apart from those memories, nothing had really concerned Maman since she had come to Les Bugues. Sometimes she thought of my marriage, but more out of curiosity than anxiety. I think that long ago Maman had secretly, in her heart, abandoned her children. She had done it in her own way, full of grace, because she could only stand herself in deprivation, but the most innocent kind. I had always known her to be fascinated by the shimmering of the passing days; no matter whether they'd been somber or gay, she had never dreamed of lamenting or celebrating them. She was neither happy nor unhappy, she wasn't with us; she was with the passing time, in harmony with it.

When by chance I had Maman to myself, I always marveled at her utter grace. Tonight, I forgot the others who were waiting for me in the next room. I didn't see her eyes, which were looking down. Round, soft wrinkles ran over her firm face, a sign that she had aged and that her life would soon end. She wasn't thinking about that. Already it was no longer Maman who was on this chair but her image. I thought of her death on a morning in the middle of summer. It was almost nice to think about, it was a simple and natural thing. We wouldn't bury her in Ziès like Jérôme, but right here, facing the beautiful valley of the Rissole.

She asked me whether I would marry Tiène. We didn't know who he was, Tiène, deep down, she said; we didn't know his family. She would really have liked to meet them at least once in order to marry me off properly.

I kissed her and told her that she was mostly curious to know what was going on with us. She didn't insist and immediately changed the subject. She told me something I already knew, that Luce had come back from Ziès with them and that she believed Nicolas was happy about it. I knew that she would have liked for me to give her my opinion on Clémence's departure and Luce's return to Les Bugues. But I had nothing to say and she remained silent too. She must have shared my opinion that it was impossible to speak about. Now that Nicolas was free after having waited so long to be so, we felt very removed from him. I had the impression that Jérôme, more than us, had kept him in Les Bugues. Maman must have felt that as much as I did. By eliminating Jérôme, Nicolas had lost his former patience and his reason to wait. And Luce had appeared at the precise moment when Nicolas was seeking a pretext for his new freedom. We didn't know exactly where it would lead him before he realized that it was in fact something other than Luce he had been waiting for all these years. Something else entirely, which cannot be reached through madness or reason. No, we didn't know anymore what Nicolas would become. It was discouraging to try to catch a glimpse of it. That's why Maman stopped questioning me and soon wanted to return to Papa. He himself called her, impatient for her to go up.

She must already have grown bored with thinking of Nicolas, angry at herself for having thought even for a moment of keeping him near her. I kissed her on her little wrinkles, on her wilted eyelids and along her forehead, at the edge of her hairline, there where she doesn't know she exudes the scent of a flower.

She walked away, then I heard her say to Papa what a nice evening they'd had.

I thought to myself that we had parents solely to be able to kiss them and smell their scent, for the pleasure of it.

I went to join the others in the workshop.

Luce and Nicolas were sitting next to each other on the divan. Luce's head was leaning against the wall, her neck exposed. Her eyes were closed, but it was as though she was still looking at something through her eyelids. Her motionless face now expressed something like a profound fatigue despite the slanted smile still on her mouth. She didn't hear what he said in her ear. She seemed to be thinking of something outside that moment. That one day she would leave Nicolas after having waited for him for so long. She must already have known it, been despairing over it in advance. She had always known it, all the while hiding it so naturally, but now that she finally had him all to herself, she could probably no longer hide it from herself.

He was hunched over her throat, his arms stiffly tensed along his body. His hands, flat on the divan, grazed Luce's hands without trying to grasp them. He seemed distracted from her, caught up in observing her face. In a muffled voice, he questioned her incessantly: "Why on horseback? So late? At night, always at night?"

He'd had a lot to drink, but not enough to abandon his slightly angry tone, nor to dare to take her in his arms. He saw that she already seemed exasperated from waiting to go off with him. I wondered whether he was living a kind of nightmare. She repeated: "I don't have my horse, you'll take me home."

She knew Nicolas too well to play at tantalizing him. The only thing she didn't know was the body of this boy who had grown up with her and with whom she had always remained close and separated by a sort of sibling modesty. He sensed that she was impatient to go off with him. That's probably why he was speaking to her so much, to keep her there, so that she would give him some respite before he went with her down the path. Her haste didn't fool him, it distressed him.

When I think about it now, I believe that Luce's desire was different from Nicolas's. It was a desire that had always been there, that she'd had the courage to admit to herself only very late. She was the one who had taught him that they desired each other and that they could conquer their brother-sister distance.

Now, in trying to stall her, Nicolas was spoiling the pleasure she surely wanted without delay, perhaps also without tomorrow.

At the end of her patience, she dragged him outside.

They didn't say goodbye to us. They left together in the hot August night.

I stayed alone in the workshop with Tiène. Seated at the piano, he was singing and lightly playing with one finger. He heard Luce and Nicolas leave, and he thought I had left too.

He thought he was alone. He hummed more loudly. I didn't dare move, and stood in the middle of the workshop without making a sound. I could see nothing but his back at the other end of the dimly lit room, his back and his neck over which his hair grew in little copper-colored specks.

For two weeks, he hadn't spoken to me. He no longer seemed interested in me. I didn't know that he sang. Hearing him, it was as though life was suddenly stripping itself of events like useless bark, to appear beneath, peaceful and strong. I had never caught him all alone. He seemed happy.

No one knew Tiène. I didn't know him either. I told myself he might soon leave Les Bugues. His departure, like his arrival, would teach me nothing about him. He was profoundly uninterested in all of our stories. He was there merely for his own pleasure, a pleasure that we would never understand, that of living with us. I must not have meant any more to him than Nicolas or Luce. Thinking about it, it was as though he had forced me never to love him, to please him only by remaining the same forever, by being no one. Soon he would leave me in Les Bugues with them, with nothing.

I asked myself suddenly whether his departure was of great importance, whether deep down I wanted him to leave right away. I think that, without admitting it to myself, I wanted to chase him away, in that very moment, from Les Bugues.

We were alone together. Now the night was black through the windows. A sweet, thick scent of magnolias entered the room. The wind wasn't blowing. Between the swaths of total silence, we could have heard the magnolia flowers detaching from the trees and falling into the darkness.

I left Tiène at the piano. He noticed nothing. I wouldn't have been able to join him as I had intended. Every night that was my intention; every day I pushed it to the next day, without ever daring to do it. I told myself that I would go sleep on the hill of Ziès in Clément's hut. Clément had constructed it for rainy days. It's at the top of the hill, and from there, in the morning, you can see the entire plain of the Rissole all the way to Ziès.

Crossing the courtyard, I could still hear Tiène. His song followed me for a while; after the courtyard, it still tried to walk at my side, then it was gone. After the gate, at the edge of the path: August alone.

August bloomed after the trees, once they were all in flower, overnight. How to remain at the height of this month, linger for a moment in this August-before-September vertigo? Woods, ripe plains, warmed cliffs, stood still in a supernatural stupor at the heart of which September and October were brewing. The ditches of Les Bugues smelled of rot, of August that carries within it all the scents of the months.

I was no one, I had neither name nor face. Moving through August, I was: nothing. My steps made no sound, nothing signaled that I was there, I disturbed nothing. At the bottom of the ravines, frogs full of life croaked, educated in August things, in death things.

We didn't know Tiène. One morning, four months ago, he came here and asked to see Nicolas. It was an April morning. I was cutting the buds off the tobacco trees. He stopped on the path: "Nicolas Veyrenattes, does he live here?" He looked tall and had a face and voice that were completely unfamiliar to me. He didn't seem cold despite the wind. It looked as though he had slept in the forest and just come out of it. He wore a well-made suit; I had not seen him arrive; his hands were empty.

It was the first time a stranger had come to Les Bugues. Apart from the three families that surround us and stop by from time to time, no one ever comes to see us.

I looked at my hands, all blackened with tobacco. I was wearing an old pair of Papa's pants that I wear for this type of work. I felt a little ashamed. I approached him. The wind was tousling my hair and prevented me from seeing him clearly. A cool breeze was blowing in the white sun. He had probably forgotten his question. I reminded him: "Why Nicolas Veyrenattes? He does live here, but why do you want to see him?" He didn't respond, but asked if I would be cutting tobacco for long. "The whole morning," I said, "and maybe the beginning of the afternoon."

"And what does Nicolas Veyrenattes do during that time?" I told him he plows the fields with his father. He asked me again whether I cut tobacco very often, whether I liked this work. I answered each of his questions without suspecting a thing. It wasn't really a conversation. It rolled through mundane and specific things that didn't seem to hold any significance. He seemed distracted and I too responded distractedly; his questions were so simple that they didn't require any reflection before answering, so I could examine him freely while we spoke.

"I'll take you to Nicolas." "Yes, good," he said. And calmly, he walked by my side. As we walked through the woods, the breeze blew harder. We said nothing and only the sound of our steps crashed into the silence of the morning. From time to time, he would look at me and think, his head down. His profile was so beautiful that his features seemed to tear painfully away from you. I saw that he was still very young. Bent forward in this way, his face tensed and relaxed in turn.

"Are you Francine Veyrenattes? I came to live near Nicolas and you. I'm looking for room and board around here." I asked him why. "I met your brother in Périgueux.

We chatted for a while. He told me about himself, about his sister. It was last year; after that I went on a trip, I couldn't come straightaway. But now I won't be leaving here for some time." It was obvious he was not telling the truth. Nicolas would surely have spoken to me about this meeting. If he had hidden it from me, it must have been because he deemed me incapable of understanding. Immediately I imagined he had come to hide, from a crime, from a hundred things. But no guess matched the very strange appearance of this young man. I informed him that we were about to arrive at the field where Nicolas was working. But first he had to tell me why he was here rather than elsewhere. "I wanted to meet you." We stopped face-to-face, just a step apart. The silence of the forest whistled in our ears. I warned him: it was a funny idea, here it would always be as if there were no one around him. He said no, that it wasn't true, and anyway, even if that was the case, he wanted to remain near us. "There's Sunday morning when there's nothing to do. There's each night and it's long, the winter, and no cafés around, no neighbors." He smiled. What I was saying seemed to amuse him. "And you all?" he said. "And you?" Us, we were used to it. For us, boredom was not an issue, not even on Sundays. As for me, it was different. I had not chosen to stay here, I had not chosen to leave either. He said: "How so?" I couldn't explain it to him properly; I'd still never had the thought that I could have not lived in Les Bugues. That was why I didn't get bored.

At the Ziès crossroads, I pointed out the field where Nicolas was working. That same night, he and Maman agreed on a rate for his room and board. He went back to get his things in Périgueux and returned the next day. That was eight months ago. I asked Nicolas why he had never spoken to me about Tiène. He hadn't forgotten him but hadn't wanted to tell me we were going to take in his friend until he was sure he was coming, because he didn't want me to be disappointed.

From time to time, I go up to Tiène's room. I forget for weeks at a time why he came to live in Les Bugues, then impatience takes over once more. I want to know more about him, to know everything. I can't help myself. I need to know why he's here. He came to spend some months with us, but he could have spent them elsewhere. He never responds in a convincing way, he repeats that nothing spurred him to come except what Nicolas had told him about Les Bugues, about me. One night, I said: "If you left without telling me, I would die." And I believe it sometimes. He laughed and suddenly became like a child against whom no harm can be done. He claimed it would take a lot more for me to die. I asked him whether he found me beautiful. If he found me beautiful, I could have believed that he stayed because I was a girl he desired. But he didn't respond to this either. He couldn't have told me I was beautiful, obviously, but at least that he liked me. If I had that small certainty, I believe I could know Tiène better, make him up based on my own face. But he has never told me that, or that he loves me. He takes me in his arms and we remain entwined on his bed. I stop asking questions. We can no longer talk. The unknowing between us transforms slowly. We hear it come undone and turn into an understanding that nails us to the spot. I don't know anymore why I questioned him.

A few days after Jérôme's funeral, I was able to go up and see Tiène after dinner. He asked me what I had done with my day. I hadn't done anything in particular, I had taken care of Noël. He always wanted to know more about me, too. He questioned me right away: "Jérôme is dead; are you the one who told Nicolas that he was Clémence's lover?" Yes. He knew that but probably wanted to hear me say it. Had I not foreseen that Nicolas would kill him? No, although I'd had high hopes for the fight, I had not foreseen this. But that Jérôme would be gone? It had crossed my mind, but how exactly, I didn't know, I hadn't thought about it.

"He'd been living here for twenty years; did you think he would leave on his own? He owned nothing and no one other than you would have taken him in. And, as you know, he would never have decided to go on his own." Yes, probably, but I hadn't considered it. Or that Jérôme might have killed Nicolas? No, I knew very well that no, the times when Jérôme came to work with us, I had carefully measured each of their strengths.

Could I still have prevented them from fighting, on that morning? Couldn't I have separated them on the train tracks? And why had I gone there, if not to try and fix things?

He surprised me with his questions; I told him that I hadn't expected him to ask me such things. I felt like going home. He held me back as he never had before, grabbing my shoulders and forcing me to sit down. He had lost his habitual calm. His face expressed intense curiosity and a bit of anger. I felt happy suddenly. I couldn't think about what he had just said to me, I thought only of those hands.

But he continued: I had to speak to him sincerely and not give him an explanation for my actions that would appease him, because, he added, he was not looking for any particular explanation for Jérôme's death. I responded that the truth was difficult to parse out in this case. But maybe if he helped me and proposed a version that he found plausible, I would have a basis for comparison; I could see more clearly inside me; all my lies, even involuntary, would fall away on their own; then it would be much easier to figure out why I had delivered Jérôme to Nicolas.

"You knew they would fight because you encouraged Nicolas to provoke Jérôme. You knew very well why you wanted it to occur from the moment you denounced Jérôme and Clémence. I want to know whether this intention remained clear within you throughout everything that happened after you decided to pit Nicolas and Jérôme against each other."

In that moment, as when I had brought him Noël the night Clémence left, I believed Tiène loved me. I couldn't explain the curiosity he had about me any other way. I told myself that his indifference was possibly just a sham, that maybe he was asking me these questions because he had been trying in vain to answer them for himself since the fight. He thought about me, he was interested in me. Perhaps it was only me who kept him in Les Bugues. I wanted him to speak, to speak to me the whole night about me, without forcing me to answer.

I answered that I didn't know. I hadn't had any specific intention except to see Nicolas reach his limit. That was all.

He almost shouted: This was unacceptable, I had to force myself to think.

I couldn't tell what he wanted from me. I couldn't think of an answer. But I was no longer afraid that he disliked me. It wasn't possible, he couldn't dislike me; on the contrary he must like me even more. I had the feeling that he was questioning me in order to know just how much he might like me. And this, at the same time, made him furious at himself.

"Obviously, you, you didn't hate Jérôme?" No, I couldn't take him seriously, so I couldn't hate him either. I, for example, could not have killed him. Even despite all his wrongdoing and the pain he had inflicted. If we were hidden away for the last twenty years, it was because of him; if we lived in embarrassment, it was because of him. But I admitted that even these reasons didn't seem decisive. No existence seemed desirable to me, and the one we led probably suited me as well as any other. So I would never have killed Jérôme. But on the other hand, I knew that Nicolas, he could do it. So hadn't I made my brother do what I couldn't have done myself? No, as for that, no, I maintained. "And you believed Nicolas would end up doing it?" Of course, Tiène knew, Nicolas would never have been able to live unless Jérôme disappeared, and it had to be by his own hand. He was as convinced as I was, Jérôme and Clémence had to disappear from Nicolas's life.

Did I know that Luce Barragues and Nicolas . . . ? Yes, I knew it, I had suspected that Luce would return to Les Bugues sooner or later once Clémence left. Luce Barragues precisely enclosed Nicolas's life. When I told him this, Tiène became distracted, as if he were suddenly bored. His tone grew calmer. "Is there someone in your life who could be compared to Luce?" There was no use lying to him, he would have guessed it, he guessed all of my answers in advance better than I did. I looked at his hands, which were at the same height as my face. I felt that they held me entirely, in that moment, between their tight fingers. I told him the truth, that sometimes I believed he, Tiène, could be, but that he himself did not believe it completely; if sometimes I got that impression, as I did then, I quickly saw that it was not true.

Tiène hushed up for a moment. He didn't insist. Then he continued to ask me questions.

Had I done this solely out of love for Nicolas; did I love him enough for that?

Sure, I loved him just the way he was. I was the only person who could do him good. He didn't know and would never know it. He thought himself impressive and wild, but I knew he would never have had the courage to kill Jérôme if I had not assured him that it was his duty. Indeed, I was convinced enough to allow him this illusion. Tiène did not know just how much I loved Nicolas.

"Nicolas will soon feel remorse, remorse is real," Tiène told me, "and no one can escape it. Even strong people, people like you." I realized that Tiène was smiling. He was poking fun.

I answered that I was surprised to find him so shortsighted. Remorse seemed to me an easy vanity to fight off, a kind of importance people still granted to themselves. You could stop yourself from having any; I would have no remorse, I was sure of it. As for Nicolas, I would see to his. I would never admit to him what my role had been in this affair. He needed the impression of great responsibility too badly. It was only by attributing to himself an authority of this kind, unquestionable, that he could be completely happy with Luce Barragues. I did not think it would last past the autumn with her. Unless maybe she was expecting his child. In that case, the solution would find itself. In the opposite case, it would be better for Nicolas, who would then finally be able to leave Les Bugues.

Tiène laughed, he told me that I was a little girl; he held me to him on his bed and started to stroke my hair.

"You have to look further than Nicolas's best interest in order to understand." Probably. Maybe it was simply the desire to change my existence that had pushed me to denounce Jérôme. But I couldn't be certain.

"When did this idea come to you?" I told him: it was around a month ago, one night. I couldn't sleep and I could hear Jérôme and Clémence in the room, next to mine. All at once, I felt disgusted, I decided we had put up with them for too long.

Tiène smiled: "So they kept you awake?" I admitted to him that some nights I waited for him to come meet me in my room and I couldn't fall asleep. I listened for the slightest sound in the house, that's how I happened to hear Jérôme and Clémence; who actually made as little sound as possible. I knew they had been sleeping together for several months, but it was only in waiting for Tiène long hours at night that I had been forced to think about it and had found the situation unbearable.

Tiène told me that the issue of lying wasn't relevant to me, that I had been reflecting a certain truth, that it might have seemed feigned, but he knew it was pure and coherent. He spoke in a dreamy tone. I didn't quite understand what he meant. He added that I was not a liar, that if I said false things it was only because I was still seeking the truth.

Maybe he was right, but suddenly I didn't care. I had never supposed that he could be wrong. Maybe he had also been right about not coming to see me for several months. I had just forgotten for a while that this night, too, I was the one who had come to meet him. He may have known a lot about me, but in this moment, he had no idea what I was thinking. After waiting for him night after night, I had decided to come and find him. He had just discovered many things about me, and he was smiling at being able to know them, but this was less interesting to me than the fact that I'd succeeded in spending a part of the night by his side. Now he slowly caressed my face; I could feel the warm palms of his hands on my cheeks and forehead. He didn't know that it was possible only because I had wanted it. He must have thought at that moment that he was not entirely separate from Jérôme's death and been surprised to see me so skillfully avoid admitting it to myself. I too had just discovered that I had been disgusted by Jérôme and Clémence only because I was alone while they were together. But I told myself that I would deal with that later. For the moment, it was an insignificant thing compared to Tiène's real hand running distractedly over my face.

We chatted some more. He asked me whether I thought Jérôme had taken a long time to die. No, I didn't think so. On the contrary, his agony had lasted just long enough for us to have time to get used to the idea that it was done, and done by Nicolas. He agreed with me.

He wanted to know if I was tired, if I wanted to sleep next to him in his bed. It seemed to me that he was the one who was tired. He held me to him. He was completely calm. His hand paused in my hair and we remained still. He asked that I forget all of his questions. Why had he questioned me? "I need to know everything about you. It was necessary. Now it's all fine." We remained a while longer pressed quietly against each other, eyes closed, knowing we were together. Then Tiène sought my mouth, he laid me down against him, his legs wrapped around mine and locked them in place.

September arrived, the days came and went, long, short. I was very tired: all of the work, Clémence's and my own, and Noël, who had to be cared for. Then came those September days that rounded out nicely with the black angles of the night. When the shadows arrived, nothing more to do in the fields and we headed back . . . Always earlier, and we knew it would be always earlier until Christmas. Three months . . .

Tiène was there, at my side, in the fields; at my side, at the table. Nicolas didn't notice that it was no longer summer. Yellowing September arrived with its smell of extinguished fire. He traversed it in great cavalcades, on Mâ, near Luce. Nicolas worked with us very little. Sometimes in the fields we saw them pass by on the paths, riding their horses. It was still very hot. She was wearing a silk dress; his arms were bare, his chest uncovered. They chatted, they laughed, they whipped their horses. We also glimpsed them on the hillsides, on the roads, on the banks of the Rissole. At night, they tied up their horses and slept together in the forest. Sometimes Nicolas brought her to his room in Les Bugues. Rarely.

Three weeks went by like this. Then Nicolas started working again. It was still hot. The men remained in the courtyard to repair the tools, to cut the wood. They repaired the sections of the wall that were in a bad state, they replaced some tiles in the dining room.

Nicolas had several projects. He and Tiène cleaned one of the rooms in the outbuildings, carefully plastered and whitewashed it. Nicolas wanted to make it into a dairy store. He said it would bring us some money. We needed money, and we could have it. We would have it. With our meadows, we could get more cows, make some butter, sell it in Périgueux, purchase a cart, fatten the calves. I think Tiène lent him a large sum of money. Nicolas went to Périgueux to buy a cream separator and a churn. Once back, he told me I would take charge of it so I could learn, so I could know how to guide the servants later on when we had them, which would happen soon. He needed money, he said. I thought to myself that he intended to marry Luce Barragues. I said nothing to Nicolas. I had no objection, but I guessed that this idea had come only to him. She surely hadn't thought of it. I made the butter for a few weeks, alone in the dairy store. Every Tuesday people came to buy it from Périgueux, and indeed, with our two cows, it was a good amount of money each time.

Tiène worked with Nicolas. He listened to his projects with a certain interest; he had lent him some money without worrying about whether he would get it back one day. He came down later than usual. In his room, I would find several open books scattered on his bed; he would fall asleep among them. During that entire period, he must have felt bored in Les Bugues, but he still didn't talk about leaving.

He went to Périgueux several times. He took nothing with him and always returned the next day.

Once they stopped taking their daily strolls, Luce Barragues came every night to eat dinner at our house. Nicolas would go off with her afterward; he no longer slept in Les Bugues. He would return in the morning and work relentlessly all day. She would arrive around seven on her horse. She always wore new dresses. Her hair was loose around her shoulders. I found her beautiful, always more beautiful. Each night was a celebration thanks to her visits.

As soon as she arrived, Nicolas went to find her and help her get off her horse. He wouldn't leave her side. He followed her into the kitchen when she helped me prepare dinner. One time I caught them in the hallway. Nicolas, crouching, was biting her legs. She lifted her silk dress brusquely and Nicolas kissed her thighs, caressed them with his face and hair. She was pressed against the wall, her eyes closed, her body stiff. Her expression was grave and drawn.

We made many wonderful meals in honor of Luce Barragues. Nicolas didn't even notice that the cooking had changed. He always made Luce Barragues speak and listened to her with the same kind of delirious attention as in the first days. She spoke with ease; I found everything she said enthralling. She spoke of her life with her little brothers and her father. At every opportunity, she said how much she loved her father. During her entire youth she had remained a lodger in Périgueux. That had been very difficult. On two occasions she had managed to escape. Eventually they had been forced to send her back. She also spoke of her mother's death in the same tranquil tone. From time to time, she would notice Nicolas watching her and caress his arm gently. That's when he would take her hand; he must not have always realized the force of this gesture. Luce would grimace, irritated, and sometimes also laugh. Each night, we got her to speak about herself, to tell us the same things; she kept returning to them. We never stopped being interested in her. All of us except Nicolas were bored those days in Les Bugues.

Tiène didn't seem to take as much of an interest in Luce's stories. Sometimes this annoyed me. I'd say: "Tiène? Tiène isn't listening to you, Luce." I don't know why I wanted to call out Tiène. Luce would stop short. Tiène would smile kindly and apologize. But Luce's laugh would become less natural.

. . .

Soon, after maybe three weeks, I noticed that while she was pretending to have no interest in Tiène, Luce spoke readily only when he was there. Then I realized that she left reluctantly with Nicolas in the evening. She always waited until the last minute to head back. Our parents went to sleep; I went up to my room. Tiène, Nicolas, and Luce stayed in the workshop until very late. It was only when Tiène went up to his room that I heard the others cross the courtyard. Nicolas didn't seem to notice a thing, not that she avoided looking at Tiène at the table, not that he himself tired her with his constant, heavy attention. It's true that her boredom was barely visible at first. I thought I was inventing it. But once Tiène went to spend a few days in Périgueux. Luce came as usual. When she didn't see him return at dinnertime, she was unable to hide her anxiety. But she assumed he was just running late. When she noticed that I wasn't setting his place at the table, she must have felt fear. Not disappointment, but a real fear that he was gone for good before she'd had the chance to find out if he liked her. Skillfully, she brought the conversation to Tiène. She asked me how he had ended up staying with us, why he was here, what he was doing and where he usually slept. I told her the truth, that I didn't know any more than she did and that he would probably leave the same way he had come, with no reason. That he was a friend of Nicolas's, that he had probably liked Les Bugues in the beginning but that I had noticed for some time now that he was bored. Without intending to, I managed to feed Luce's concern to the point of causing her distress. I wanted to know whether she had admitted to herself that she loved Tiène, and also how insignificant she thought I was to be able to speak about it to me in such a way, so carelessly. And then, I don't remember why, I said that Tiène was returning the day after next. Luce went back to being quite happy. I think that up until that night even she didn't know what she hoped for from Tiène. She didn't realize that I had guessed it before her.

It was during an outing organized by Nicolas at the beginning of September that everything was revealed.

"We'll go swimming two kilometers from here," Nicolas had decided. I would bring Noël; Papa and Maman would come too. We would have a picnic after our swim.

Such an outing, for us, was rare. We planned it several days in advance.

With Luce's help, I prepared the picnic the day before. I remember that afternoon clearly. The men were in the courtyard cutting wood. The sound of the axes, steady and monotonous, reached us in the kitchen. We seemed happy, as if a kind of peacefulness was slowly settling into the house. It was no longer the unnerving calm that had followed Jérôme's death; this calm left us with our spirits free and allowed us to work with a pleasure so light we could barely feel it.

But Luce, Luce couldn't help herself, she looked overjoyed. She was thinking about the picnic the next day; she knew that Tiène was in the courtyard and could come in at any moment to ask us for a drink. At times she grabbed me playfully around my waist, but it bothered me a bit. I was sure she was doing it to see whether my body was beautiful, whether I was as slim and toned as she was. She told me: "You're tall, Françou, almost as tall as Tiène, but you've worked too hard in the fields, you're sturdy like a man."

I went along with it, I liked her. Because she was pride, pride personified. The kind I knew I would always be incapable of.

I think she still cared about Nicolas at that moment. But she couldn't bear the indifference of anyone around her. Certainly she doubted Tiène's love for me. I understood that she must have thought no one, except my brother, could ever love me. And strangely this brought me closer to her. Because while I resented her a little for believing it, I couldn't deny that I believed it too. From the day she started to think it was possible, she began to spy on me. She must have suspected that I held a certain importance, I don't know what kind, that I hid away from everyone but Tiène.

. . .

We didn't really know how to have fun, Nicolas and I; we had always gone swimming alone and we felt embarrassed. But Luce was quick to drag my brother and Tiène along. The three of them went for a swim while I took care of making Noël comfortable on a blanket near my parents. When I couldn't see them anymore, I got into the water too. I thought I'd go up the Rissole until I found them.

But once I was in the water, I chose to go down the river instead of joining them. I was not a very good swimmer, and I found it easier to go with the current than against it.

The water was cold. I soon felt as fresh, as alive, as it was. I started to swim with an unfamiliar ease. Without knowing it I had probably been waiting for a long time to go down the stream of the Rissole on a beautiful afternoon.

Tiène wasn't there, he had gone the other way, but it was as if I were swimming toward him, though I knew he could not be in this direction. I would glimpse him on the bank; he would say: "You're so beautiful when you swim." After a while, I didn't know if I was dreaming, it was as though I had been lulled to sleep by my steady swim; I no longer dared to look above the water, as if my wanting to catch him there watching me was going to drive him away. The current was strong, and it overtook me. I had no trouble swimming. The sun was high and the surface of the river burst into yellow and blue mirrors before my eyes. Without trying to see them, through the wickers I glimpsed the still shadows of cows moving slowly through the valley. I passed two small children who were fishing. I was probably the one who had warmed up the water; it became softer and softer to sink into, more and more familiar.

In the end, I struggled to breathe and felt the desire to stop swimming. I got out of the water. I no longer expected to see Tiène. I knew that I was alone. They were behind a small forest that concealed them. I couldn't even see Papa and Maman.

I lay down on the grass in the sun. I was tired. I had almost forgotten Nicolas's little party. There was plenty of time. The afternoon was long, after all, and they could start eating without me. I had gotten up at five in the morning to make the butter so I could go with them. I felt myself slowly falling asleep. My fatigue was mine, mine alone, I couldn't share it with anyone, I didn't want anyone near me. I had drawn it close to my body while swimming and now it enveloped me, as secure, as entangled, as sleep. It was not deceptive, my fatigue; it was like the sun above my head, full and round. I no longer wanted to move at all, and yet at the same time I wanted to leave and never see them again. Not because they had left me alone or because I was bored, but because I wanted proof that I was capable of doing it, I wanted the memory that I had been capable of doing it. It was because my body was so heavy with fatigue that my thoughts went off so freely, so light.

I thought about the sea, unknown to me. My eyes were closed, but I was not asleep. I knew I was not yet asleep. I thought about the sea, the various ways people had told me it was endless. I wanted in that moment to look at something that, like my fatigue, was unchanging and endless. I fell asleep.

Tiène and I climbed up on two black Mâs who galloped through a blue emptiness above the water. This, in fact, did not end or begin. All beginnings and all endings were lost all around us. Everywhere the sea emptied, escaped into the slits of the sky. The Mâs galloped daringly and for no reason. I said: "Finally, this is it; we're at the sea." The wind whistled. Tiène was happy. In reality he wasn't there. It was just his laugh at my side.

They called me, and I woke up. I had fallen asleep just minutes ago. I quickly crossed the river and ran over to them. They didn't ask me where I was coming from. That's how it had been since Jérôme's death, everyone pretended not to know I existed. Nicolas barely spoke to me, and everyone imitated him. It was as if I reminded them of something unpleasant that they forgot the moment I was gone. I think they willingly accepted that

Nicolas had killed Jérôme, since they knew I was the one who had pushed him to do so. This way, Nicolas could feel no remorse, it was I who should feel it. Even if they were now free and happy, I still had to feel it. That afternoon, it became clear to me that I was with them as someone who had to ask forgiveness for simply daring to be there at all.

We laid out a tablecloth at Papa's feet and started to open the bags. At first we didn't really know what to talk about. Since Jérôme's death, we had been together only when obliged, at meals or in the fields, for example.

Tiène was sitting next to Papa. Smoking, he informed him of the projects under way at home, at work. He said: "For the bricks, we could get them from Périgueux via the Ziès truck driver." I could tell he was embarrassed because he spoke hastily about things he could have spoken about at any other time. But Papa and Maman were so at ease that little by little, just by looking at them, we began to feel at ease too. We stopped trying to talk nonsense in order to seem natural. Peace of mind settled over us all. We started eating.

Luce helped me unfold the packets of food. When we were done, she rose abruptly. She asked Nicolas to lie down and sprawled with her head on his chest. Then she called to me affectionately: "Will you fix us something to eat, Françou? We swam and swam. Will you, Françou?"

She was wearing a white bathing suit and her legs poked out, slightly spread apart, long, smooth, still wet.

She seemed weary, as if unable to move at all. Her legs and arms were lifeless around her, abandoned. Her golden face was shining, gleaming, dried by the sun. Her eyes were closed, but through her lashes she was watching Tiène. She had positioned herself across from him so he would be forced to see her and so Nicolas wouldn't notice that she was watching him. By placing her head on Nicolas's chest, she could rest easy, yes, he would have no idea of her little game. Nicolas saw only her, he played with her wet hair, gently ran his hand down her throat, under her small swimsuit, over her bare stomach. She wanted Tiène to know how much Nicolas adored her. She seemed ecstatic, paralyzed by the view of Tiène's eyes on her body. On her smiling face, her desire to capture Tiène's attention was clear. She had abandoned all prudishness, she seemed to have forgotten we were there. Nicolas was the only one who didn't notice. Even Papa and Maman looked at her without understanding, a little surprised.

I cut the cakes and brought some to Luce and Nicolas. Nicolas said: "Thank you, my little Françou." It was the first time since Jérôme's death that he had called me by that name. He also said that the cakes were very good. From these few words I understood that he was perfectly happy, since it cost him so little to easily return to me in front of everyone.

As usual when Luce was with us, the meal was very cheerful.

I remember Maman saying all of a sudden that we shouldn't eat too much if we were going to keep swimming. Maman is always silent, and from time to time, in order to seem interested in the conversation, she utters such phrases without thinking.

"We have plenty of time to eat and swim," said Luce. She added that Madame Veyrenattes couldn't honestly think we would die of indigestion. I was a little annoyed on Maman's behalf. We laughed, not really making fun of her, but because we realized that despite all the changes that had taken place in Les Bugues of late, Maman had remained the same, just as distracted and trying just as hard not to seem so. Papa was laughing very hard, tears in his eyes. What Maman had said hadn't been very funny, but it had abruptly made us remember her. We laughed with pleasure and surprise at still having her with us. She was wearing the same clothes as the day of the funeral, the same taffeta dress. But she seemed younger to me than she did then. She was a bit embarrassed by our cheerfulness, then she joined in our laughter, as if she also had to admit that she was charming. Papa seemed younger than usual too. Papa is small, he has a rosy complexion and blue eyes. His coarse hair is white and like Noël's, all over the place. On that day he wore a white suit.

When we finished our meal, I fed Noël. Ever since Clémence had left, I alone had taken care of him. Nicolas was so consumed by Luce that he no longer paid the smallest bit of attention to his son. Despite his few teeth, Noël took a very long time to eat his cake. He played at spitting the bites back out onto my hand, then burst into laughter so intense he lost his breath.

I stood a little apart from the others. On my left, Papa and Maman had started speaking again in low voices. The town of R. was not far from here. The others chatted a few meters away; I had my back to them and I couldn't hear their conversation clearly. Noël irritated me with his laughter. He took his time playing; that was my only task, to amuse him. He was still playing, he had his whole life to play. I thought Clémence would be back soon and that maybe it would be best to give her back this child. But for now, I had to feed him. Time passed, an unknown amount of time I could not bear to feel pass.

"Nicolas Veyrenattes, does he live here?"

Tiène was next to me. I hadn't heard him approach.

I let go of Noël and lay down at Tiène's feet. I was laughing silently, and he laughed, too. Then he said:

"Do you like cutting tobacco? And what does Nicolas Veyrenattes do during that time?"

I answered: "He plows the fields with his father."

He grabbed me under my arms and lifted me. We found ourselves standing next to each other. Tiène was so beautiful! I hadn't gotten a good look earlier. He was stunning. He looked at me from beneath his hair and looked only at me. His body was surprising in its beauty. His feet, his hands, his face, had become unfamiliar now that he was naked. They were no longer separated from his blond body, agile, seemingly smoothed by the water of rivers, the wind. It needed no clothes. It was draped in sunshine. I asked myself then whether it was possible to love Tiène. How could I have found the slightest resemblance to myself in him? What was Tiène doing here, in Les Bugues? What did he want from me? What was he doing here, alive? How could he be alive? I suddenly looked at him without recognizing him, without love, there in his unapproachable solitude.

But right then, without warning me, he grabbed me by the hand and dragged me along. We ran by the river, slowly, then fast, we distanced ourselves from the others. The moment we left them, Nicolas and Luce stood back up, they didn't even have time to consider following us. Nicolas smiled, a little surprised. Luce didn't understand what was happening at first. Then she cried: "Tiène, what are you doing? Come back for us, Tiène! Tiène . . . Françou . . ." Her voice was shrill, mean. We were already far away. I turned and saw her, her arms at her sides, her face deformed, unrecognizable. But Tiène didn't want to go back. We plunged into the river and swam together side by side. When we stopped, the others were no longer in sight. I told Tiène that we should have waited for them. Luce would certainly make a scene with Nicolas, and this evening he was bound to notice something. I added that he would probably be forced to leave Les Bugues, since this situation could not go on. He wasn't listening to me, he was still smiling, attentive only to my lips as I spoke, to my naked body near his. What I was saying became more and more unintelligible the longer his silence went on.

Tiène lay down at my side. His body touched all of mine. He said: "Be quiet."

A long moment passed. The others must have gone home. Now Nicolas had to know. It was done; I felt at ease.

The sun cooled down and sometimes, when I opened my eyes, I saw the blue shadow of the hill of Ziès extending into the valley.

Tiène's face was sad, darkened by shallow grooves, the purple lids half closed. He didn't know I was watching him. His firm, golden torso was like a tree trunk. Right down to his fingers and toes, a force was forging its path. At one point, he took my hand: "You probably know that I'll be leaving soon?" I said yes, I knew. He cast off my hand in anger.

It was then that I started to crave Tiène in my mind, to desire his naked warmth against mine, against my face, his face disfigured with desire. I know it was from that day on for him, too, that he stopped himself from coming down to my room, knowing all the while that I was waiting for him there.

He didn't come until three days after Nicolas's picnic.

. . .

Luce Barragues returned for dinner as usual. She tried to be friendly and not show that she had come only to see Tiène. I don't know what occurred after our outing, but Nicolas could no longer be fooled.

From that moment on, he began to speak about Jérôme. He insisted especially on Jérôme's good qualities, as if he were trying to provoke indignation in us for what he had done. He reminded us of a young and pleasant Jérôme, the one who had come to R. in Belgium and walked with us through the town when we were little. He said that Jérôme's life seemed to him the saddest of lives because he knew it well. He even asked for the key to his uncle's room in order to dig through his papers. But for all the trouble he went to, no one really believed that he was tormented by what he had done.

He no longer worked with us at all. He loitered around waiting for Luce all day, and when she was there, he struggled to seem at ease and spoke out of turn, seizing any opportunity to say Jérôme's name.

One night, she didn't come to dinner. Nicolas didn't come to the table. He hopped on Mâ and rode to her house. The next day, she returned. But the following days, she kept us waiting again, in the evening, without warning. Nicolas went off and didn't return until morning. As for us, we knew it was useless now to hold her back.

She stopped coming altogether. Nicolas spent entire nights roaming around her house. She probably didn't want to see him anymore. He returned only in the morning and stayed in bed all day long. When I brought him something to eat, he didn't seem to understand what I wanted from him. The last days, he asked me whether I thought she would return. I told him she would not. He didn't believe it. He no longer wanted to see Tiène, and yet he must have missed his friend. He wasn't sure it was because of Tiène that Luce didn't love him anymore. In fact he didn't care, he had no more shame. Every night, he got up, he got dressed, he hopped on Mâ and went off again in front of all of us who no longer even dared to look at him.

I can't remember thinking about anything during that time. I worked all day long. At night Tiène came down to my room.

. . .

One night Clémence knocked at my bedroom window. I let her in. She wore the same dress and carried the same suitcase as the night she left. Her face was all white, pierced only by her little brown eyes turned shiny with tears. She had just walked from Ziès to Les Bugues barefoot in the night. Blinded by the light, she didn't seem to notice that Tiène was there.

"Noël, where's Noël?"

I went to get him from Tiène's room, where he had been sleeping since his mother left. I counted; it had been two months that Clémence had been gone. I wrapped him up asleep in his blanket and brought him to her on my bed. When she saw him, she started to tremble, then she knelt before him, without crying, without saying a thing, and she watched him attentively. I noticed that Tiène was a little pale. He was looking out the window. Noël woke, cried a bit. She waited for him to fall back asleep and undid the blanket to see him naked. She said: "He's grown." She turned toward us with her face twisted and cracked by a smile. She asked whether I was the one who had taken care of him, whether he was doing well. I answered yes to all of her questions. I stood there behind her, next to Tiène. She thanked me for taking care of Noël: "Thank you for everything you're doing for me."

We said nothing to her, and time passed. She continued to contemplate her son in silence for a long while, then, abruptly, she was no longer afraid to wake him. She nibbled his hands and feet; right after, she kissed him carefully. At one point she turned around:

"I'm disturbing you. I'm sorry."

Because we didn't answer, she probably thought we were eager for her to leave, and she started to sob. She took Noël out of his blanket and crushed him against her chest. It seemed she was hungry for him, she moaned with rage at not being able to get enough of him. Noël made a face and started to whine again. She was screaming that she wanted to die with him and that she would take him far from the others, from us. Her face was repulsive and red, her lips wet with kisses.

"After all, if I wanted to, I'd take him. You people couldn't stop me."

She forgot us, she glued her lips to Noël's cheek, and very gently, her eyes closed, she whispered in his ear that he was her little Noël, her little boy, the only thing she had on this earth. Then she lashed out at us again: "I didn't know what I was doing, you had no right to take him from me. I was a martyr in Périgueux, and for nothing. Anybody else would have been forgiven, but me, I couldn't stay, nobody liked me here and that's why I was chased away."

She said we had endured her when she was still a maid, but from the moment she married Nicolas no one could stand her anymore. She had figured it out a long time ago, she added. We were terrible people, nobody knew how we had made her suffer, bad people who concealed our true nature . . .

She stood up, Noël in her arms. She paced through the room. She had a voice I didn't recognize, confident and vulgar. She seemed taller and larger, as if at last she were occupying her place of air. She rocked Noël mechanically. From time to time, hiding against the wall, she stopped cold and spoke to him under her breath. Already I knew what she was getting at because each time she passed before me, she stooped her back and avoided raising her eyes so as not to see me, so she could hold on to all of her courage.

Abruptly she stopped and, with her shoulders hunched, she hissed:

"All of this, you're the one who did it, you, all on your own."

Then she remained planted there, weak, moaning, carrying Noël at arm's length. Now she wanted to set him down. I didn't know what to say, and she got scared. She put Noël on the bed. She took her suitcase and said in a gentle voice:

"I had come to stay, but after what I've told you, that would be impossible."

I told her she could stay in Les Bugues if she wanted. She threw herself at me and laughed nervously. Her face had become stupid again.

"Now you tell me!"

She squeezed me in her arms.

"Oh, it's not true, it's not possible."

She could go to bed. It was late, she could go back up to her room with Noël.

"Oh! Yes, right away, but give me the time to gather myself."

And Nicolas? Had Nicolas forgiven her?

You see, now she would be perfect; in two months she'd had the time to reflect and she knew Nicolas better. I told her not to wait on Nicolas, that he was rarely home. I wasn't sure whether he'd kick her out tomorrow, but for now she could go up to her room with Noël. For a few days, maybe she should hide from Nicolas. I needed time to inform him that she had returned. In the event that Nicolas didn't want anything to do with her, she could take Noël to Périgueux.

She went shaky: "What's going on?"

"Nothing." Except that I didn't think Nicolas wanted to see her again.

She didn't insist. She went up with Noël in her arms.

. . .

Clémence stayed. I spoke to Nicolas about her the next morning. He told me that she'd better stay for Noël. He was not mad at her at all. He had never been mad at her.

For three days after Clémence's return, we didn't see him in Les Bugues. We assumed he was at Luce's, and nobody worried about his absence. Luce later told Tiène that she hadn't seen him during those three days.

It wasn't until the morning of the third day that Clémence found Nicolas's crushed body on the train tracks. His arms were stretched out before him, his feet apart. He looked like a dead bird.

PART TWO

Every night a train passes through Ziès on its way to T., an Atlantic beach. Our family often spoke of going there. The conversation frequently revolved around this idea on certain winter nights. But money was always lacking—or a real willingness to go.

It was yesterday after lunch. Tiène and I were leaning over the terrace parapet, and I told him that I wanted to go to T. at least once in my life. I hadn't thought about it seriously, but Tiène told me that I had to go, and quickly, before the season was over, as soon as tomorrow. He would give me the money.

I woke early. The train is at eight twenty-five; it stops for one minute in Ziès. With so much grief it's hard to figure out what you want or don't want. Not to mention the scruples of leaving Tiène alone with my parents. I wasn't sure I wanted to go. Now I hear myself walking determinedly down the road. Tiène was right to suggest it. I will probably never have the chance to go on this trip again. We haven't done anything in Les Bugues since Nicolas's death. For the first time, we find that work can wait a little longer. Aside from Clément, everyone lazes about. Incidentally there's little to do in September. We're waiting for the sharecroppers, they're coming in fifteen days. Until then I have time to go to T. . . . The sea. You still want to know it. Tiène knows it. Nicolas won't have seen it.

The train stops at every station, empties, and fills back up regularly. Sometimes, between two stations, it runs a little faster.

The people get on and off and take their seats on the benches. They are sure about arriving, sure about wanting to leave. I can't stop myself from staring at them.

Not one of them is going to T. They are for the most part farmers going from one village to another. A woman in her forties has sat down next to me. She's wearing all black. Her hands, worn from washing dishes, rest on her lap. Her gaze is absent. A small ivory brooch holds a scarf with flying pleats around her neck. She smells like dairy and lamb. No doubt she's seen to everything she left behind: the clean Saturday house, the wood in the hangar, the little ones washed, dressed, the raked corner of the cemetery. Before her: the harvests, the seasons, reaped in advance, order.

On each side of the train kilometers of trees, fields, homes pass by. The people watch them pass in a peaceful stupor.

The end of summer. They're talking about it in the compartment. They're saying that it's the first real autumn Sunday.

After waiting three hours at the station, I took the other train. I arrived in T. at nightfall. I was told of a boardinghouse that is supposed to be decent, inexpensive, overlooking the sea.

It's cool out, the night is dark. Bands of young people move through the streets in gusts of laughter. I can hear the sea. I've heard it before somewhere, this sound; it reminds me of a sound I know. It was while trying to figure out where I had heard it before and what it reminded me of that I noticed I had arrived in T. The feet before me, beneath me, behind me, they are mine, the hands at my sides that leave and rejoin the shadows in the succession of streetlights, I smile . . . How could I not be smiling? I'm on vacation, I came to see the sea. In the streets, it's really me, I feel tightly confined by my shadow, which I watch lengthen, topple, return to me. I feel tenderness and gratitude for the me who has brought me to the sea. I have not yet caught a glimpse of it, the sea, because of the houses. Tomorrow I'll have the time. I'm hungry. Here is the boardinghouse I was told about.

"It's quite late for a young lady," says the manager. She's alone behind her register; large, her face worn by fatigue. She asks me if I'm staying long in T. Suddenly I think of the old Veyrenattes who have turned into babies and stay in bed all day. (But I have to make an effort to remember.

As with Jérôme's screams when I went to fetch the doctor a month ago.) Tiène will soon get tired of looking after them. Two weeks, I say, two weeks, no more.

The room is big and very bright. Most of the tables are against the walls. In the middle, there are two small ones, fully set, waiting for the clients or guests who arrive late.

I'll probably sit at one of these tables for dinner. There. I was hungry after all. The two large bay windows that are now closed must overlook the sea. The murmur going through town earlier is more defined here. The bar is empty. The door is closed. It must be late. They made me go through the back earlier; in the kitchen, two maids were having dinner. The one serving me comes back over, still chewing. A few guests are playing cards, the others are chatting. They seem very young. The women keep saying: "I'm going to bed!" The men gently protest, take them by the arm, force them to sit back down. Indeed, they gladly consent.

The air smells of blush and skin burnt by the sun. On the booth there are beautiful bare arms, taut breasts beneath red, yellow, white scarves. They laugh. They laugh about everything. They try each time to laugh even harder about everything. Behind their sporadic laughter you hear the blue and hoarse sound of the sea.

I'm done with dinner. All is well. It's already been an hour.

Their fun is milder. They yawn, they stretch out in their booths. They're tired, they probably swam, laughed, ran on the beach, and now they're sleepy. I am not tired, I am not sleepy. They shouldn't go up to sleep yet, they should stay near me so that I can watch them. I find them very beautiful. They're in good health. They half-open their lips, and automatically golden nonsense spills from their mouths. On all of their faces is the same laugh. They look alike. There are many of them and it's hard to tell them apart. I am at ease here, confined with them. It's neither time for me to sleep nor the moment to move. They shouldn't move either. If just one of them leaves, only one, the first, I will suffer. For the moment, I am well. All is well. It's that time, the end of a day. If they leave, it will be the start of something else, of what I don't know, of a night probably. All is well. But if they go, I don't know what I'll become. I'm scared to wait again for the next day, scared to cross on my own this mournful headland that separates each day from the next.

But thankfully, they're not thinking of leaving yet. They play cards, they continue to talk. I remain hopeful that they'll forget to go to bed.

At some point, one of them, with black hair and eyes, broke away from their group and came toward me; he said a few words of welcome. He offered me a cigarette and invited me to come sit at their table. The others waited for my response, impatient for me to join them. I looked at the man: he looked friendly and eager to chat. But I was unable to accept his cigarette. I said how much I regretted not being able to stay up with them, that I was tired from the trip, very tired; I came from far away.

I went up to bed. So it goes. I had nothing to give or say to them. Really, they shouldn't have offered me that cigarette. It was an invitation to amuse them, and I don't know, it's not true, I can't. I don't know why all of a sudden I would have rather been killed than reach for that cigarette. And yet he was friendly and I was grateful to him for thinking of me.

Here, in my room, it's me. It's as if she no longer knows it's her. She sees herself in the mirrored armoire; she's a tall girl with blond hair, yellowed by the sun, a tan face. In the bedroom, she takes up too much space. From the very small open suitcase, she pulls out three blouses to look natural before the girl watching her. Though she avoids seeing herself, she sees what she's doing in the mirrored armoire.

The bedroom is very small, the table bare. The walls are very fragile. Someone strong would topple them by knocking into them. On the yellow wallpaper falls a great vertical rain of parallel black stripes. The bed is well made, covered with a white blanket. In front of the table, a chair. She sits. What to do? Seventeen days ago today Nicolas died. It's true. Some time already, and it keeps on going.

. . .

I think it was on the second night that it happened. I hadn't realized the night before. I hadn't noticed that when the door of the mirrored armoire was ajar, the entire bed was reflected in it. I was lying down when I caught sight of myself lying down in the mirrored armoire. I looked at myself. The face that I saw was smiling in a way that was both inviting and timid. In its eyes, two puddles of shadow were dancing and its mouth was firmly closed. I didn't recognize myself. I got up and shut the door of the armoire. Then, even though it was closed, I felt as though the mirror still contained within its thickness an unknown character, at once fraternal and full of hatred, who was silently contesting my identity. I didn't know anymore which was more closely related to me, this character or my body lying down here, familiar. Who was I, whom had I taken myself for until now? Even my name did not reassure me. I couldn't locate myself in the image I had just come upon. I floated around her, so close, but there existed between us something like the impossibility of uniting. I found myself attached to her by a faint memory, a thread that could snap from one second to the next, and then I would plunge into madness.

What's more, once the girl in the mirror vanished from my eyes, the entire bedroom seemed to be populated by an endless circle of companions just like her. I sensed them calling to me from all sides. Around me a silent phantasmagoria had been unleashed. With a wild quickness—I didn't dare look, but I sensed them—a crowd of forms must have appeared, tried me on, disappeared straightaway, as though obliterated by not fitting me. I needed to find a way to grab hold of one, not just anyone, one alone, the one I had been accustomed to up to that point, whose arms had until now allowed me to eat, her legs to walk, the lower half of her face to smile. But she was mixed into the others. She disappeared, reappeared, taunting me. I, on the other hand, still existed somewhere. But it was impossible for me to make the necessary effort to find myself again. No matter how many times I remembered the recent events in Les Bugues, it was another who had lived them, who had replaced me forever, waiting for tonight. And if I didn't want to go mad, I had to find her again, she who had lived them, my sister, and embrace her. Les Bugues became distorted in spurts of successive images, cold, foreign. I didn't recognize them anymore. I didn't remember them anymore. I, that night, reduced to myself alone, had other memories. And yet even those, huddled in the dark, only tried to creep into my memory, to make themselves seen, to breathe for a moment. Memories from before me, from before my memories.

It was by accident that I glimpsed myself in the mirror without trying to. I didn't seek out the image I knew of myself. I had lost the memory of my face. I saw it there for the first time. I knew in that moment that I existed.

I've existed for twenty-five years. I was very little, then I grew and reached my size, the size I am now and that

I'll be forever. I could have died in one of the thousand ways people die, and yet I managed to cover twenty-five years of life, I am still alive, not yet dead. I breathe. From my nostrils emanates real breath, wet and warm. Without trying, I managed to die of nothing. It advances stubbornly, what seems halted, in this moment: my life. I hear the beat of my heart, and the palms of my hands feel like they belong to me: to me, to the one who endures my discovery in this moment. In this very moment as I hurtle with the armies of things—men, women, beasts, wheat, months . . .

My life: a fruit I must have eaten some of without tasting it, without realizing it, distractedly. I am not responsible for this age or for this image. You recognize it. It must be mine. I'm all right with that. I can't do anything differently. I am that girl, there, once and for all and forever. I started to be her twenty-five years ago. I can't even hold myself in my arms. I am bound to this waist I cannot encircle. My mouth, and the sound of my laugh, never will I know them. Yet I wish I could embrace the girl that I am and love her.

I look like other women. I'm a woman of rather ordinary appearance, I know. My age is an average age. You could say that I'm still young. My past, only others could tell me whether it's interesting. I don't know. It's made up of days and things that I cannot bring myself to believe really happened to me. It's my past, it's my story. I can't bring myself to be interested in it because it's my own.

It's as though only tomorrow will really begin to include my past. Starting tomorrow night, time will count. For the moment, every past other than mine belongs to me more. Tiène's past or Nicolas's past, for example. It's because no one warned me that I would live. If I had known that one day I would have a story, I would have chosen it, I would have lived with more care to make it beautiful and true so that I would like it. Now it's too late. This story has begun, it leads me where it likes, I don't know where and I have no say in it. Even though I try to push it away, it follows me; everything falls into place, everything decomposes in memory, and nothing new can be invented.

I could be a thousand times different from what I am, and at the same time be all those thousand differences on my own. Yet I am only this girl who looks at herself in this moment and nothing more. And I still have perhaps another thirty years to live, thirty Octobers, thirty Augusts between this moment and the end of my life. I am forever trapped by this story, this face, this body, this head.

. . .

Three days I've been here, and nothing is happening. I have nothing to do. Tiène is far away. Now I can glimpse what it meant to love, and to suffer, and also to be interested in the story of others. It wasn't serious. Only I didn't know it. Now I know that what is more serious is not to do anything and let the others figure it out.

It's calm here. In Les Bugues I was restless, for years. I always had to think about not spending too much, about hail, about Nicolas's future. As if he hadn't needed me to be able to die how he wanted. I do nothing and I speak to no one. It's strange, I'm not bored. I don't think about getting bored. Boredom is far away, vague. I already know it will come. But first you have to dig it a place.

Near the sea there are birds I'm not familiar with. They pass very high in the sky. At times they descend to the rocks. They're white as salt. Sometimes I see them resting on their stomachs on the crests of the waves. Never do you see them up close. They are birds of the sea. Their cries are plaintive and smooth. At night, when I can't sleep, I think I hear them, but it's the wind that I hear. It comes in one piece from the high seas and crashes into the firm things of the earth. For the ear listening to the night, the wind and the cries of the birds are the same. You can't stop yourself from thinking about them, thinking about their snowy broods in the hollow of the stones beaten by the sea.

At night, when I can't sleep, I think about how Nicolas is dead, how at this moment he's in the little Ziès cemetery, forevermore. How I'm lying in this bed, still alive for an indefinite amount of time. But those thoughts are always the same, and you can distract yourself from them easily. You believe you're thinking about the same thing, and you realize that you're thinking about something else. But it might as well be the same thing. It's always the same. I begin by thinking about Nicolas, and I always end up thinking about those birds that sleep in the wind's passage, in the holes of the stones beaten by the sea.

. . .

Sometimes I think of Tiène. When men pass me on the beach, half naked, I think of Tiène's body. It's then that I think: I am a woman. I am alive as a woman, not as just anything, as a woman only. I wouldn't dare admit that until now I had hoped to be alive as other species too. To run down the hill one day like Clément's dog. To spread my branches one day like the magnolia tree in the courtyard. I never admitted to myself that it seemed impossible to be a dog in disguise, a tree in disguise. Now I tell myself the truth, that things are quite different.

What a hypocrite I am! You can't see the abyss that's there, between my legs. Anyone who discovered it would think it had just opened beneath him, through him. It is perfidious and innocent. It is a thing that always waits for someone to come, someone who is nothing but a culmination of something else. And yet the bottom of this abyss is also a refuge, the only refuge from the sky and one of the last walls on earth. Nothing I can do. I am nothing next to it. But it is within me, clinging inside me, evident on my face.

I forget it easily, but it remains bound to the thought of Tiène. Tiène is the man I love. He will be perhaps the only one to whom I can offer this cool well for the rest of my life. There are all the others that I will never know. But it's the thought of Tiène that made me realize that it's mine, that it can be somebody's, be mine, be Tiène's. Before knowing it, I felt it vaguely inside me like something empty or maybe something full, full of a total ignorance. It emitted an empty cry to no one. Since then a force has grown there, against which I am defenseless; a thought has settled there, inside me, against me, around a shape, which is always the same, the shape of Tiène.

And yet there are all the others. They exist. With their smiles. I won't see them seek me out. I won't watch them discover me. I won't listen to them flatten against me in all of their confidence and rise again in confusion, like those birds who rise again on the pebbled beach the wind has thrust them upon.

I am the woman of one man. Tiène alone is irreplaceable because all the others, no matter how many, would never console me after Tiène, would only push me to seek him more and more.

I love Tiène. It is no longer something that might happen. It has already happened. It's done. I love. I love Tiène. Even from afar, I feel that I no longer want anyone but him. The things that until now I thought were the most important to me have vanished. But I still have this desire for Tiène. It's there, dammed up between my hips, a kind of wisdom that is wiser than me and knows better than me what I want.

. . .

The sun soon finished its race. The sea is still a uniform green and the horizon is clear. And yet it is unmistakable. The breeze rises and the sea rushes up.

For as long as I can remember, I've always worked hard alongside Papa and Maman. I couldn't do anything else. And I always had to sleep tight, even on windy and stormy nights, while thinking of the next day's sun. I had to keep watch with the wind, which demands to be heard. Was always reasonable, good, a virgin until twenty-five. I had to welcome the men who came with their insistent smiles or just their beautiful arms. And the others, my parents, I had to not love them to the point of waiting for them to give me orders, pleasure, sadness. Since they awaited some kind of change from the outside only and abandoned me for the slightest reason, I don't know. For death, madness, travel.

I would of course still have arrived at the same point. Time is old and still would have been, but at the time it was radiant and I had no idea. I was a girl stingy with my body, with my life. And now time is old. Once you lose the ability to forget, you are permanently deprived of a certain life. This is no doubt what it means to leave childhood behind.

This life, I lived it through Nicolas. He lived my childhood in my place. I was five years older than him and very small. I was always amazed to see him smaller than me, weaker and more willing to make believe. One day I found him asleep at the edge of a field, exhausted with joy. I watched over him until sunset, surrounded by the bees, the snakes, the twilight. He slept alone in the field that overlooks the valley of the Rissole. He was six. Beneath his breath, the blades of grass closest to his head would tilt slightly, barely, regularly. I carried him home in my arms.

I took very little care of him. Most of the time, he was running through fields on his own. He was dirty and always poorly dressed. What I loved was to find him suddenly abandoned in the depths of his childhood.

Now he's dead. He lay down on the railroad, along the tracks, his head burning with a love that was not for me against their coolness. He watched the train arrive, and perhaps he forgot when he saw it that he had lain there to die. As for me, at that moment, I was sleeping with Tiène, in the same bed, naked against him. Already, already, I was not very concerned about whether he would live as long as me, him, Nicolas.

His death, easier and worse than the prospect of his death. It can no longer happen. This is the great difference I carry within me. I myself have lost a layer, lost the fate that wrapped me up like a garment. I am naked.

The sun has set. For a few minutes it illuminated the sea, which went all saffron on the surface, greener and colder than ever beneath its crust of light. The sea is everywhere now that the sun has set.

. . .

I looked at my dress thrown on the bed in the room. My breasts have given it two breasts, my arms, two arms; at the pointed elbow, the armhole is gaping. I had never noticed that I wore my clothes out. I wear them out. The dress gleams at the lower back, at the waist. Beneath the armpits, it's stained with sweat. I felt the desire to leave, to leave this dress in my place. To disappear, abduct myself.

(Her face felt very warm, she put her head on the pillow, she felt like dying then and there.)

The first nights, I intimidated myself. I met my hands everywhere, my face in the mirrors, my body on my path. I couldn't really tell what was mine, which is why I kept thinking back to Nicolas, to remember who I really was and to reassemble the pieces of me that were scattered across the room.

On the beach, alone, in the sun, it's so different. You can feel your heart beating all the way to your fingers, a filling and unfilling of this density between the ribs, shut inside. My bare leg, lying on the sand, I don't recognize it, but I recognize my beating heart.

. . .

It's two in the afternoon. You can't imagine how long it takes, how slowly a day is inscribed in the sky. I'm here the entire day. Like yesterday. But no . . .

You couldn't say I miss Tiène. I don't think of him, of seeing him again. And yet this scent of the sea that reaches me on the beach in a sharp, fresh breath, I recognize it. It's a scent of elsewhere. It's the scent of deprivation, of being deprived of Tiène, who sleeps and dreams and pays no mind to me. The wind that comes from the edge of the horizon comes from Tiène's chest, more wind than before, after touching something like his blood. I recognize this wild sound, the taste of salt and steel, the scent of war.

Tiène was sleeping. I listened to him breathe. I thought about the trips. The ones Tiène had taken. The ones I hadn't taken. The ones I would never take, with or without Tiène. The wind leaving his nostrils was damp with the spray that fogs all departures. Tiène had left me, was dreaming of leaving me. He was a man sleeping alongside a woman. A kind of victim who could not make up his mind to leave her. I felt sorry for him. But I leaned over his hair and smelled the scent of dry grass, which was the smell of the whole bed. The smell of: now. This moment proved to me that Tiène was in fact there, nestled in the depths of oblivion, but there nonetheless. This moment was his body, which I could caress. His bare neck you wanted to grab with your hands without clenching. His eyes that, with one shout, I could have brought back to the surface of wakefulness. His two wrinkles that encircled his half-open mouth and made him more real than his voice. There was nothing to do, nothing to say, and yet my heart was filled with cries of pity and cries of victory.

. . .

Often around the middle of the afternoon, the wind rises. The sea whitens. Sometimes the sun hides. All at once the shadows are gone. And everything pales as if stricken with fear.

Two hours of stillness under the sun, doing nothing, just looking at the sea, always the same: then my head can no longer do anything, it can no longer choose one thought over another and retain it. Thoughts float at the same level. They appear and disappear: wrecks out there on the sea. They have lost the appearance and the meaning that usually makes them recognizable, all while keeping their form in a manner at once absurd and unforgettable.

The thought of my person is also cold and distant. It is somewhere outside me, peaceful and drowsy like one of those things under the sun. I am a certain form in which a certain history that is not mine has been poured. I wear it, this seriousness and indifference with which you assume what is not yours. I do think, however, that an event might occur that would be so entirely mine that I could fully inhabit it. Then I would claim my defeats, my insignificance, and even this instant. But until then, there's no use trying.

The little crate that arrived on the beach the other day was holding on by just a few nails, some jutting out, rusted and bent. On one of the boards you could make out the words "oranges" and "Californ." It must have been opened by a cargo ship's crew, emptied of its oranges, and thrown out to sea. It was there, rid of what it had been used to contain. And yet it endured, more useless than ever and more than ever a crate-for-oranges. The ebbing tide took it away. It went off again on the crest of the waves, all alive and delirious. Between its four boards was a genuine story, a genuine lack of history that shouted in the face of the sky.

You look at the bird, always the same one, scraping the sky with circles soft and white. A cloud passes over the sea and leaves a smudge of night that disappears just as fast. On my finger is the jade ring from Grandmother Veyrenattes, who was in Borneo and whose death has been recalled only three times in the twenty years since—the third time being now.

Why Tiène? Why him and not a thousand others just like him? In this moment you prefer everything that you didn't prefer when you preferred Tiène. You can do without touching him, waiting for him, wondering whether he's thinking about you at this very moment. That's how it is under the sun.

Nothing holds you back, nothing pushes you forward, even slightly. Not even the sorrow of no longer feeling the icy wake of the thought of Nicolas in your stomach.

. . .

It's always Nicolas's eyes that I remember when I remember he's dead. Not very big, purple in the sun; gold particles swimming in them more or less visibly depending on the intensity of the light. In the center, the black pupil, the opening to a cave where it was always dark. Lashes like paintbrushes surrounded them and carefully protected them from dust, from the too-vivid sun. And those eyes allowed Nicolas to see. At night, he closed them to sleep. Then he opened them back up in the morning and used them all day long. A smooth wetness soaked their surface and the lids would slide over them so naturally that Nicolas never suspected he could have felt them. From the terrace, Nicolas could see the entire valley of the Rissole with those eyes, and at the same time, the sky that covered it. Just as he was able to see Luce's eyes and her immense mouth approaching his own. Until the last minute, his eyes saw. The last thing was two shining rails inscribed in the dark cave.

Now they're in the coffin with all the rest, with the feet, the hair. Nicolas killed them. Through them, Nicolas was inundated by the day, by joy, by love, too. They were more than Nicolas. Perhaps such eyes should not have been given to him, he who killed them.

. . .

What has passed and what will come is entombed in the sea, which is dancing, dancing, right now, beyond all things past, beyond all things to come. Some mornings by the sea, I feel that I too, as I walk, am dancing. Days of light sun, wet sand, foam that smells like fish.

In the sun. My thighs in my hands. I caress them. The warm palms of these hands meet the coolness of these happy thighs. From these exposed armpits rises the smell of fresh humus, which is mine. In the shadow of my skin, my flesh works, devours the days one after the next with a never-ending voracity. Everything that has happened to me has drowned in my skin. It's not much, to tell the truth, just what has happened to me personally; for example, all the images my eyes have seen since my birth, all of them, all of them. For my eyes are connected to my body through my neck, and I can't help it, they couldn't have seen in the place of Nicolas's eyes, for example. I have only the existence of this body to house my own existence and to prove to myself that I have only begun to exist. This body has worked, worked, cried over Nicolas's death, attempted to die under Tiène. It ages. Deep down, I like that. There is no forgetting. It has not been forgotten. I feel proud when I think about it, and a kind of respect for it for suffering this common fate so honestly. It's beautiful, my twenty-five-year-old body. These feet are tough, accomplished, these feet have walked. It's here in this little field of flesh that everything has happened and everything will happen. That one day my death will bite and latch on with its mouth until together we form a pile of stones.

For now, my death is a little beast inside me and we live together in perfect harmony. It doesn't show itself. It's only when I think about it that I feel it nestled in the depths of my belly. When it shows itself, I will recognize it. There's the first hot day in April. The one when Tiène kisses you for the first time. Others, and that one. You know everything in advance. It will have the icy muzzle of young cats, a burning breath. We will finally get a close look at one another.

Of course it's possible that you'll die rather quickly, but we must still have the time to really meet again.

My own death; you mustn't block that hole through which the head relieves itself of everything inside it, including its own sediment. As it drains, a violent wind blows and carries all of you with it. If you willingly let yourself flee, without being stingy over the smallest detail, you'll quickly find yourself a long way away, distracted, restored, saved, and you'll observe: "Here, people are swimming, a little farther on a girl is staring at the sea, even farther, a lighthouse."

But at that moment you have to move a leg or simply a finger. (And she is the one who has to die.)

. . .

Once upon a time there was a family who lived apart from the world in a place I know well. They lived in a big house that barely contained them. They were poor.

They worked. So poor that they were forced to never leave one another and to eat at the same table every day of the year. There the ones who worked the most and those who didn't do much lived side by side. The old who didn't think before speaking. The young who didn't speak so freely. And in the end, they had come to believe that some of them hated each other.

In summer, these people would burst through the walls of their home and each go off on the June paths. They would come home late and weary, which allowed them to see one another very little, to sleep soundly, sometimes to dream.

In winter, you could have seen them through the window (but in reality, no one saw them ever), their faces drawn with distraction, all around the same fire. They always worked in the same fields on the same days. The seasons passed. Their existence never changed and seemed like it never would. Nevertheless, this household lived in a patient fantasy. They dreamt of finding a way to part ways forever. They didn't love one another as much as they thought, nor did they hate one another as much. But they found themselves united by poverty, by marriage, by the fact that no real reason to leave each other presented itself, except for their desire for something to happen. But as time went on, this desire found every excuse not to happen. As can occur when you allow the expectation to grow so much that it can never find the right pretext.

I lived off their expectations so much that in the end I was the one who tried to tear open this dreamskin with my nails.

I awaited what would follow: the moment when these fantasies would surge from the night, when these people would grab hold of each other, kiss the mouth of the most valiant among them. But their dreams had carried them into a shadow so ancient that they staggered in the light. One morning the sun rose, but over their corpses, and there was nothing to see. The house closed back up. You will no longer see their gazes gathered around the same fires. That's it.

Only I still exist with this knowledge.

What does it mean to know or not know something? Which lesson from that knowing can untangle what is happening to me, face-to-face with this void that rises before my eyes in ever more immense waves, in ever more devouring clarity?

. . .

On the sea, everywhere at once, flowers burst. I think I hear them growing on their stems a thousand meters below. The ocean spits its lifeblood into these hatchings of foam. I traveled to the hot and muddy vestibules of the earth that spat me out from its depths. And now I've arrived. You come to the surface. There's enough room for the entire ocean to croak in the sun, for each part of the water to marry the form of the air and ripen around it. My own form observes them. I am flower. All the parts of my body have burst under the power of the day, my fingers burst from the palm of my hand, my legs, my stomach, and all the way to my hair, my head. I feel the proud weariness of being born, of having come to the end of this birth. Before me, there was nothing in my place. Now there is me in place of nothing. It's a difficult inheritance. Hence the feeling that I am an air thief. Now you know it, and you welcome being in the world. I steal my place from the air, but I am happy. Here. Here I am. I sprawl. It's beautiful out. I am flour in the sun.

. . .

One night I was by the sea. I wanted it to touch me with its foam. I lay down a few steps away. It didn't come immediately. It was the time of the tide. At first it didn't pay attention to what was lying there on the beach. Then I saw it become surprised, naive, it even sniffed me. At last it slid its cold finger through my hair.

I entered the sea all the way to where the waves burst. You had to cross this wall curved like a smooth jaw, the palate you see when a mouth prepares to swallow, not yet closed. The wave is only slightly less high than a man. But that doesn't decide the winner; you must fight with this height that fights with no head and no fingers. It will grab you from below and drag you to the bottom thirty kilometers away, turn you over and swallow you. The moment you traverse it: you emerge in a naked fear, the universe of fear. The crest of the wave slaps you, the eyes are two burning holes, the feet and hands have merged with the water, impossible to lift them, they are knotted to the water, lost, yet wanting to return to those limbs of innocence itself (the ones you used to take your first steps, flights, thefts, they cry: I haven't done anything, I haven't done anything . . .). It's very dark out, you can't see anything but calm in the gleams. You are eye to eye with the sea for the first time. Eyes know with just one look. It wants you straightaway, roaring with desire. It is your own death, your old guardian. So this is what has been following you since your birth, spying on you, sleeping slyly at your side, now showing itself with this shamelessness, with these howls?

You must advance with the last of your power, what is left once even breath has escaped you; with the power of thought.

After the wave it's calm; that's where the sea does not yet seem to know that it stops. Facing the sky, you find the air, its weight. You are a peaceful beast with breathing lungs, with sliding eyes that smooth the sky from one horizon to the other without ever looking at it. Thirty meters of water separate you from it all: from yesterday and tomorrow, from the others and from the self you will meet in your room momentarily. You are but a peaceful beast with breathing lungs. Little by little, that which thinks gets wet, soaks itself in opacity, an opacity always more wet, more calm, more rhythmic. You are seawater.

But quickly, suddenly: thought. It returns, chokes on fear, bangs its head, now so large (so large that the sea could fit inside it); suddenly it's scared to be inside a dead skull. And so you move your feet and your hands, which are back to being your friends. You slide intelligently with the sea until it casts you onto the beach.

When I return to the boardinghouse, I watch it from my window, it, the sea, it, death. It is the one that's caged now. I smile at it. I was a little girl. Now I'm all grown.

. . .

I've been in T. for nine days. I still have some of the money Tiène gave me. I'm lying on the beach as I do every day, thinking I still have time ahead of me. The man with black eyes, I watched him approach. I allowed him to "keep me company." I told him to sit with me. He did so immediately. I sat down in my turn. He's thirty, with a haggard face. The collar of city people has stained his neck, his hands are thin and his eyes tired from the bright sun. This man likes me. While I watched him intently, he seemed less sure of himself. He offered me a cigarette. I told him I don't smoke. He probably remembered liking me; now he wasn't so sure. He didn't know what to say after that. He turned his head toward the sea and declared that the weather was beautiful for early October. Then he asked me whether I would stay in T. long. The truth is, I didn't know. "End of September, it's dead around here." This thought did not sadden him. He continued to watch the sea, probably thinking of what to say to me next. What did he mean: dead? He told me that at the end of October, and even earlier, it was too cold to go swimming, that the people left, that the trains were scarce, the hotels closed up. And the rain. The sea clogged up with fog, the empty beaches, the wind. In two, three weeks at the latest. He was watching the sun, the bathers, the green sea, he was someone who had lived through many summers and knew how it went. "We have to wait until next year now, summer vacation goes by fast." Only next summer possessed virtues that this one, like all summers past, did not. His hands, crossed over his knees, fiddled distractedly. His dry lips sliced his face with a sad streak.

I asked him to explain how the end announced itself. Whether he already glimpsed on the water or in the sky some sign of the end of the season, since he was familiar with it.

"Except for the mornings and the nights, which are cooler, you could almost forget it's not August anymore." Which didn't mean that the weather would stay good; it would probably turn rotten all at once, he added.

He was still staring at the sea with the same distracted eye; I wished we were face-to-face so I could see if he was lying.

"And so, since I only have twenty-one days of summer vacation every year because I take eight days during

Easter, I think it was bold to take them in September. Family circumstances prevented me from coming earlier, but I don't hate it when there are fewer people. You're more looked after in a hotel and in a way it's more relaxing."

Then he glanced at me timidly, suddenly smaller. He said that he "too" enjoyed solitude, that people are bad, so selfish. At the boardinghouse, he felt it clearly, they were trying to hold on to the last September customers, whereas in August! Had I been here in August? No? Well in August, the owner sure cared a lot about her customers! The dishes arrived cold, the service was awful. So really in a way he didn't regret coming so late. (One more glance at me.)

I would have liked for him to leave, but at the same time I continued to question him, to listen to him.

I asked why he returned to T. if this boardinghouse wasn't to his liking. He said: "What can I say, I'm used to it and everywhere else it's the same, so why not." His eye got wide. I thought about his eye, how useful it was to him, he used it not to trip in the night and not to break his leg, his precious leg, and to cut his steak in the special way he liked, and to . . . and to . . . I thought to myself that every city man in every city is equipped with a similar eye, for the convenience of getting around. If I'd had a little pocketknife, some courage and enough strength, I would have liked to extract his eye and watch him stagger on the beach, so that he would always remember the sky above us right now, blue, blue, blue. Some clouds skirted it in the distance, drifting slowly.

So what did he think in the end? What I wanted was his opinion: Would the season be over soon? He looked at the sea, the horizon, he who knew, bounced his shoulders: "Believe me if you want, be aware that I could be wrong, but I do believe that this beautiful weather won't be over so soon."

I wasn't listening. A laugh rose from my loins to my face. I sprawled, I felt too much pleasure to stay seated. I had just witnessed a moment of the funereal bacchanal that erupted with the cymbals of the wind: the houses were closing up, the sailors were getting lost, the empty trains were rattling, and I, a stranger, chased off by the whip of the wind, I . . .

It had closed back up. The mute sea was still dancing like a young virgin with swollen limbs.

The man seemed encouraged by all these questions. He remembered that he liked me now. He worked for a wholesale candy company. As he lit his cigarette, he started to tell me about his life. Many misfortunes he'd suffered. He was the one who placed the orders with the retailers, but this important job was only attained after years of fighting with the commercial director who was a force to be reckoned with.

I noticed that night was falling. I asked him to excuse me, to leave me be. He wanted to know whether he could see me again the next day. I admitted that tomorrow I had hoped to be alone. "I bored you with all these stories, I'm sorry, I get carried away when I talk." He stood. I avoided answering him. "I know I was boring, but it's nice to speak to someone who understands." Was I here every night? He would come swim here. I warned him, this spot was dangerous. He regained his arrogance: "All the more reason—I'm not afraid, I'll come swim here. Goodbye, mademoiselle." He went off with a whistle, his suit open. But he felt me watching him; his stride was awkward, and at times his feet almost crashed into each other.

The following days, he often walked in front of me as I pretended to sleep, but without stopping, without daring to swim either.

. . .

We followed Jérôme. Nicolas was drenched in sweat and his eyes gleamed in his wet face. It was still very early. A summer dawn was stretching, tawny and dark, at the edges of the valley of the Rissole. Jérôme took so long to get back that when we arrived on the plateau, the sun had risen. I can still smell the scent of Nicolas's sweat mixing with that of the sleeping forest. I still crave his steaming mouth, so ignorant, so incapable of describing what had just happened. Nicolas, Nicolas. Now they're together in the little Ziès cemetery like punished children. And I'm the one on the outside. But we needed the stillness of Les

Bugues, more palpable and difficult for us to endure in August than at any other time, to smash to pieces one day. Apart from Noël, who was visibly growing up, the people of Les Bugues could only imagine themselves aging and cover themselves with a skin of silence growing thicker with each day. They could do so because each of them was waiting to be separated from the others forever, to leave. For years they waited, then what? And yet I see that I wasn't awaiting anything different than what they awaited, without knowing what. It wasn't the same for Nicolas. When I grazed him with my eyes, his dream filled me entirely. It's because I had been stared at too much by the violet absence of Nicolas's gaze that I ended up seeking a solution and pitting him against Jérôme. No one could have done it better than me, since each person had their own reasons to want it but was possessive of their reasons, not wanting to share them with anyone. We had to reach that point. Because Jérôme could have done ten times more and Nicolas still would not have been outraged. To invoke a new grievance against Jérôme repulsed him because he was interested in only one aspect of Jérôme. We simply had to reach that point. To remember that we can't ever suffer or hate to the point of believing we have the right to kill because of what has been done to us. To tell ourselves that it was impossible to find a way to punish Jérôme that would have satisfied us. And that we should not be hypocritical by hiding it from ourselves. I was only angry at Jérôme because of

Nicolas, but in the end he couldn't die on his own; I knew this was the only way of separating us from him. He had to die or risk death, he had to be afraid. No doubt I lied to Tiène when he asked me about it, or perhaps it's only now that I realize I knew it.

Immediately after Jérôme's death, Nicolas reunited with Luce. It was to be expected.

To let Clémence leave was to give Luce to Nicolas. And that suited me. In the beginning. After, we would have made her leave Les Bugues, after he was sick of her. But in the end, without meaning to, all I had managed to do was release a bird into the wind. He was a real bird, and because of me he will remain a bird eternally.

It's not a happy or an unhappy event, it's something that happened. Nicolas's death happened. It entered the house with Luce when they came back from Jérôme's burial. From that night on, Nicolas no longer belonged to us, not to Luce and not to me. I lost the words to command him to live, I lost the strength to keep him from dying. From that moment on, I lost interest in Nicolas.

Boredom is hollower than it once was, smoother, shadowless.

Nicolas should have died of love. His true valor was not in killing Jérôme, but in loving. I know that's just right, just right. It's just right like a piece of clothing that suits you, as the dawn is just right, as the night is just right.

So I watch the little crabs walk, nestling in the sand and becoming perfect pebbles. I am calm and sometimes it brings me pleasure to watch them do it, like children.

. . .

But can we ever be sure?

I remember very clearly the night when I decided to denounce them. I wasn't sleeping. I was waiting for Tiène. I was listening. It seemed that it was in fact the whispering coming from the bedroom next door that kept me from hearing the creaking of the stairs under Tiène's footsteps. As I waited, I was seized by anger. I was mad at myself for waiting for him every night, for exhausting all of my mind, all of my time with this. I felt that I was living out the most shameful moments of my existence. But at the same time, I couldn't behave any differently.

The night turned pale, then the sky blanched at the edge of the garden. The trees began to gently shake their large blue branches. A breeze slid against the wall, caressing it like an animal searching and sniffing. It was dawn.

Standing against the bars of the window, I realized that once more, all night, I had waited for Tiène. Even the two of them next door had gone to sleep a long time ago. For a brief moment I wasn't sure what to do: bang my head against the bars of the window until it broke, to empty it of the shame of my thoughts, or laugh at so much madness, at so much serious madness. But no sooner had

I thought about it than I lost my desire to laugh or despair. I forgave myself everything. I emerged little by little into a space of violent joy, for no reason. The day rose. I remember it well: the haze of the garden was suddenly streaked with long snowy paths. Almost at the same time, the barnyard roosters sang and the screeching of a wagon's wheels came down the road to Ziès. When I turned back toward the bedroom, I saw that everything had regained its shape and color, my still-made bed and, on me, my red cotton dress with gray flowers, the one that Tiène likes. The night was completely over now. I decided that I would go for a walk before eating. I was happy.

I was no longer angry at anyone, not even Tiène. I saw Tiène's face, still asleep upstairs, firm with a clenched mouth, sealed in his pleasure for sleep. I liked that Tiène was an indifferent man, so free, so wise, rid of desire.

He didn't know it yet. I was the only one who knew it. That one day I would be with him, that even his departure from Les Bugues would not stop it. He knew nothing. That he wouldn't be long in coming down. That I didn't displease him and that I even pleased him to the point of sometimes inspiring the urge to love me. Only, something was stopping him from admitting that he would come down to my room. He hid from his own eyes that I pleased him. It was this very thing that stopped everyone in Les Bugues from reaching the end of our thoughts. That stopped us from trying to get out of our laziness, something that had become, for us, more difficult to accomplish than the most indecent act. That morning, I was able to imagine doing it. I grasped that thing, held it between my fingers, precise and naked.

Les Bugues would finally break open. We would soon hear Nicolas's laughter in the large vestibule. Around the fire, there would be a great warmth. Soon, this very winter.

And then, the spring. Then others, other seasons would arrive, searing, flourishing. Ah! And Tiène would come down to my bedroom, only hiding from me to better surprise me. He would grab my waist with his rough hands; a smile would finally burst onto his face and splatter my eyes and lips with its light.

But I'm sure of nothing in the end.

Time passed. It was decided; I would speak to Nicolas tomorrow. The situation would eventually clear up.

But once I found that Nicolas had to confront Jérôme, I remember, I became sad at the idea that it would happen, perhaps as soon as the next day.

No matter the reasons I had for wanting it. I had even forgotten Tiène. As soon as I believed I had figured out how to get rid of Jérôme, I regretted how easy it was to find and choose solutions to problems with no solution, no solution if you don't want to be a liar, or vulgar, or stupid.

By morning I was already disheartened by this shameful convenience that can be found in almost all of life's circumstances.

I like to swim at night and in somewhat dangerous places. At least you know for certain what game is being played. And at night you sleep in peace, reconciled with this body that has been clever and courageous.

. . .

Days, entire days, from evening to morning, how many have you had to burn through to arrive at that afternoon? There is nothing to do. There is nothing within reach. The sea is always the same. You always believe that today you are the most alone. But it's not true; you are more alone with each day. You tell yourself every morning that you won't be able to take another step on that terrain, and at night you see that once again you have crossed a virgin space of solitude. You think of nothing important, of nothing other than what you thought of in Les Bugues, but even those thoughts become ghosts; their only use is to be thought by the mind while it thinks of nothing.

You miss Tiène, you wish you could see your parents smile, or finally listen to the story that Jérôme told so often, the one you were never able to listen to. But you start to do so well without them that it's the idea of seeing them again that frightens you. The idea of having Tiène alive again before you, for example, makes you go pale. You wish you could never have to deal with them again except as memories. You feel too great a laziness at the thought of seeing them alive again. At the hotel, I purposely return late so as not to see the other guests. When they pass by me on the beach, I wish they wouldn't recognize me or make a sign that they ever knew me. The sound of their voices is painful.

You'd like to sink in further still, hide yourself, surprise yourself alone, sneakily, see yourself all alone in a spreading silence. They are unbearable. They remind you that you too once laughed, spoke with that same ease, that raucousness, that repugnant contentment.

But everything is fine. At the end of the bleeding night, when you're done dancing and the dawn arrives and then the day, you start to think. You had to dance to be able to stop dancing, for the dance to become the most impossible thing. Your head had to be ripped apart by brass and lights for your head to want to find itself again in the fresh silence of the morning. After each ball, you'll never dance again.

After days of solitude you end up enjoying your own ignorance, alighting with it in one breath, like a good fire. So you must not trouble these slow straight flames, you must not say a word that indicates you have the slightest opinion about anything. You have to begin again in ignorance.

You look at the sea. From seeing only the sea, you wear yourself out against it, you completely wear out its four memories. You don't know what delirious ignorance will carry you away. I'm sure it could drive you mad. But you still remain between its four limbs, its arms, its legs so shy, always. And yet because you have seen only it, the sea invites you more and more unmistakably into its deaf-mute language to do something definitive. Perhaps to throw all your modesty, all your dignity, into the air like dirty laundry. You have to dare to look at yourself, you have to dance a dance for yourself alone, leave myself so I can dance myself, dance before me the triumph of my absolute ignorance of myself, my ignorance of everything.

. . .

You are sad or joyful as you please. I rest for the entire day, and sometimes at night in my room I welcome the parade of my thoughts. Always the same. You surrender to it. The window is open onto the sea. You can barely see the sky. Everything is black.

I count the years that I have left to live in the left wing of the house in Les Bugues: ten, twenty, forty years. Nothing will mark them, nothing can happen to me. I no longer want anything to happen to me. Under the shelter of the solid walls of Les Bugues: I will watch the earth cover itself back up alternately with snow, with fruit, with mud, sometimes with white betrothals, with milk, with catastrophes, with tears.

My thoughts. The more I set them aside, the more deafening than ever they return, those chatterboxes. Soon they are there, soon all in place, not one missing. I know them. Nasty things, and if there were even one missing, I would suffer.

One day I will no longer love Tiène. If I really think about it, do I even love him now? One day I will live without the memory of Tiène—an entire day without his name wetting my lips. One day I will die.

I think of that young man at the Ziès ball when I was seventeen who invited me to dance. I felt his body against mine for an entire night, breathless and tense from the extremely naive care he put into dancing well. He was the first young man who had paid me any attention since I was a girl ready to dance. I forgot about him.

One day Nicolas died. One day I woke up in a September morning, and Nicolas was buried, completely buried, in a sealed hole, completely sealed.

One day: I know that this moment is unforgettable and that I will forget it. I know that I will forget it.

You have to get some sleep. Here the café au lait is good. It's waiting for you when you walk into the room. Not like in Les Bugues, where you have to prepare it for everyone. In the morning, when you go out, the sea wind surprises you with its smack, so severe, so sweet.

. . .

I had to force Tiène to notice me, force open the door to his room. If I hadn't done it, he would never have come to me. I had to have Jérôme killed. To force Tiène's curiosity. Stretch myself alongside him completely naked on the bank of the Rissole. Force him to see me. But even then, what people say to any woman, he never said to me, that he found me beautiful. Maman, whom I asked about this, claims that I'm not ugly, that my face is regular, that my hair is thick and that I look like her little sister who was pretty and loved. But she did not tell me that I was beautiful. What everyone has the right to hear, because it's true for everyone from a certain angle at least, I never heard.

Sometimes I look at myself and I don't agree with the general opinion. At night, as long as no signal arrives from the other rooms to remind me of the world's indifference, sometimes I find myself beautiful. I feel moved by the evenness of my body. This body is real, it is real. I am a real person, I can serve as a man's wife. I can bear children and bring them into the world, for in my stomach I too have that place designed expressly to make them. I am strong, tall, there is weight to me. Under my body, the bed sags, as under Luce, or Tiène, or Nicolas. My heat surrounds me and blends into the scent of my hair. I can't get over my naked skin, fresh, ready to be touched, that perfect preparation made to welcome ordinary riches. I please myself. I am astonished that I don't please others as much as I please myself. It seems that this grace I perceive in myself is a kind that is harder to see, harder to hear. Because we are habituated to the other kind that shows itself immediately, that bursts through at the slightest pretext in the voice, in the hands, in the smile. Mine never managed to please. But it exists. It's impossible, I cannot be mistaken. When I look at my breasts, so full, so existent, no, I cannot be mistaken. In the shadow of my dresses, they continue to wait. Waiting to be breasts to which children and stares cling. They are counting on me. But it's as though I don't know how to use them.

And yet, there's Tiène. But I cannot be mistaken. It's Tiène who's mistaken. He loved a girl that I invented through trying, through trying to please him.

. . .

This morning I received a letter from Tiène.

"I did what was necessary. It was difficult to find a good sharecropper, but in the end I found some brave people: a father, a mother, three kids. They'll be here next week. It's been agreed that you'll keep the right wing of the house. They'll live on the first floor and the ground floor, on the left side. You'll have your side entrance off the esplanade between the outbuildings and the woods.

"As for your parents, I thought they could stay in their bedroom and use the dining room.

"Your father has started going out again, but he always heads for the valley where Nicolas was found. Your mother never gets out of bed. When they're together, lying down, it's clear that they are almost happy. They chat like they used to, about life in R. They shouldn't be separated, but perhaps distanced from Les Bugues, perhaps sent to the nursing home in Périgueux. I fear that your father will get back on his feet too quickly and leave your mother all alone. They speak about you sometimes, but nothing really matters to them anymore since Nicolas.

"Clément thought you weren't coming back. I reassured him and managed to keep him from leaving. Clémence left eight days ago with Noël to live in Périgueux. You will certainly have a hard time getting Noël back; unless she needs money, she won't give him up.

"Come back whenever you want. I have time to take care of moving in the sharecroppers. Now it's the end of September and there's rain. It's very beautiful. The rain doesn't last long and when the sun reappears, the smell of the undergrowth reaches all the way here. You know, it's four in the afternoon now. From the terrace where I'm writing to you, leaning on the parapet, I see more of the Rissole now that the trees have fewer leaves. I didn't know it curved so much before reaching Ziès. It glows and it's fat, almost flush with the fields. After the rain this morning, the sun is yellow like a water fruit and smells of children's hair. It makes you feel strong to be in the light and breathe in the wet air. The horizon is a harsh blue, you'll have a cold winter.

"At night I play the piano. After a little while, I sense your parents behind me. Even your mother gets up. Both of them sit on the divan and smile. Sometimes your mother speaks to me and tells me that she'd like for me to play."

. . .

Tiène: the weight of the sunlit sky that leaves you crushed by a dream. A yearning, one alone, always the same. I wish I could start everything over again, leave a perfect wake behind me, do it fast, fast, before old age, before I no longer have the desire. But at the same time, I know that I already no longer have the desire, that perhaps I never had the desire. It's horrible. There is consolation in not being able to achieve the impossible. There is no person who doesn't want it. Impossibility itself already bores me. I can't hide it from myself.

Tiène. I wish I could sleep there next to him, see nothing besides his hair, his mauve eyelids. All my anger, rub it between our two touching stomachs, surround us with a thick silence, a sense of calm. But Tiène is far away. So at this moment I want to curl up, close my eyes, die a meager little dog's death.

Perhaps I should force Tiène to marry me, not let him leave this winter, turn Tiène into a person of fortune and misfortune, make him choose our marriage over all other marriages, of all the empires choose the one already lost, every time already lost, the one we call happiness?

. . .

The window is closed. I came up to bed early and I'm not tired.

It's been ten days since I've spoken to anyone, except once to the man with the cigarette. The night is extremely silent. Everywhere, all around the room, the wind, the murmur of the sea, steps in the hallway, dogs barking below. In the bedroom, a very thick silence, and in the middle my beating heart. I still have my forever, forever beating heart. By the sea, in the middle of the day, it's different. You're in the hand of the sea. You are the pleasure of breathing it in. Within an order that does not feel, we are this insignificant disorder that feels. A thing to witness the sea. Like a gourmand, we taste the sound of our beating heart. But it could also not beat . . . Which beats for nothing. Or for a reason that today does not hold. Which beats for nothing. Every time, today is a day for nothing, which will not have its equal. You are on vacation from your self, which is useless in the meantime. So you exist for the hell of it; you are present in this present; your legs buckle, they want to move and are shaken by laughter.

In the bedroom, when the window is closed, four walls surround me like four questions, always the same: Nicolas is dead and Tiène will leave, my parents are old. And what about me? Me?

I remember. And obviously, I am appalled. As if three days earlier . . . Every time it's the same thing, laboriously I construct my solitude, the largest palace of solitude anyone's ever seen, the most impressive. And I both fear it and marvel at it.

Shutters slam. The dog barks, someone is playing with it. People laugh amidst their oh!s and ah!s. I tell myself: it's true, I was not invited to laugh. I tell myself this, even though typically I don't laugh so easily. I think of the dead who were formerly alive. However, if Nicolas were alive, if he came into the room right now, it would embarrass me. But I'd like for him to come back precisely because I know it's impossible.

It's far too late to begin to live, or to die, or to marry Tiène. You are more than old, more than death. It's much too late. As soon as you know it's true. That you really exist. That deep down death is not as bad as the absence of dying. That loving Tiène is the beginning of a poor solution to this unhappiness you wish could at least have been perfect. That you failed the most beautiful failure, the most beautiful success.

Boredom remains. Nothing can be as surprising as boredom. You think each time that you've reached the end. But it's not true. At the very end of boredom, there is always a new source of boredom. You can live off boredom. Sometimes I wake up at dawn and glimpse the night in a powerless flight with the too-corrosive whiteness of the coming day. Before the birdsong, a damp freshness enters the room, radiating from the sea, nearly stifling in its purity. Here, you cannot say. Here, it's the discovery of a new boredom. It comes from further off than yesterday. Hollowed out by one day.

I will shut myself in my palace of solitude with boredom to keep me company. Behind the frozen windows, my life will flow drop by drop, and I will save it for a long time, a long time. I say: tomorrow, because it's always tomorrow that I will enter into the Orders of Solitude, that I will have the air and manners of circumstance. For the moment, all I do is dream with the naïveté of young girls.

. . .

Each day I could die but never do I die. Each day I think I know more than yesterday, just enough to die. I forget that yesterday it was the same story. Never do I die.

And yet I know now: how moments announce themselves, approach, arrive, and envelop us for an instant in their whirlwind, how they collapse as soon as we abandon them for another impending moment. Cathedrals of wind. This monument of August, which I thought I wouldn't have enough time in my life to circle around, is already just one pebble in the gravel of memories retained in my mind. Cathedrals of wind.

Over my whole surface I am worn out by a wear for nothing, that of the time that has passed. For twenty-five years, time unspooled me like a mill. And now I'm twenty-five years old. And what once began cannot begin again. But I wish I could relive those first walks on Mâ at dawn, those, the first, not the others; to belong to Tiène a new first time, not another, in that bedroom open onto August when Nicolas was living the last hours of his last days. But no. I cannot even evade myself. Sometimes I meet myself, but there is no surprise left. Even when I'm indifferent or rude to myself, I always return to myself, always more faithfully.

I see that I have died of nothing. Surely that's why my life is this swamp where I can't remember, in my agitation, having produced anything other than the same squelch of boredom. Even if I exaggerate my pain at having lost Nicolas, I know perfectly well that Tiène had already replaced him. I have always found a way to replace everything. I always got out of trouble just in time. And yet I knew what awaited me. I didn't do it on purpose.

White beacon of my death, I recognize you, you were hope. Your light is good for my heart, fresh to my mind. You are my childhood. I understood what you meant to say, but I never burned in your light because I missed every occasion to rush in. I gave you my little brother, that torch of my little brother, and you consumed him entirely. As for me, I'm still here safe and sound in my swamps of boredom. And there wasn't, there isn't, any path other than the one you illuminate.

. . .

Sometimes I almost wish I could learn of Tiène's death. I imagine it: One morning they would leave him with me on the threshold of Les Bugues. He would die in the night like Nicolas. His cheeks would be pink with cold, his hair would be moving in the wind. Perhaps at first I would think he was alive, simply sleeping in the fresh air because it's spring. I see myself approach, I smile in the same way as the day before: thoughts of him spending the night outside. I approach again and see that his lips are green and a stare filters through his eyelids that stares at nothing. I take his hand, it is uninterested in my hand, it wants to be left alone.

Then I stop being able to think of him. I hear the scream I would emit. I would be young. My life would have served to feed that scream with all my power. I would be that scream. My age would be smashed to dust as would the world, and the Good and the Vile, and all definition. Oh! I could finally die in a scream. Without thought, without wisdom, I would be nothing but that scream of joy at having found death in a scream.

In the distance would gleam that black future. Tiène would be dead for eternity, Tiène's death would be eternally in bloom over the ashes of the world.

. . .

The man passes again and again in front of me on the beach. He wears the same suit that's too big and missing a tie. The edges of his collar are stained and his hair hasn't been cut for a long time. His stubborn face is sealed over his mouth, swollen with silence. This face is dark and often stubbly.

He appeared just now before me and looked at me out of the corner of his eye as he rushed by.

He passed me and hid behind a rock a bit farther down. A moment went by during which I waited patiently for him to emerge from his hiding place. He came out in a black bathing suit. His body was too white and hairy, he was obviously ashamed of it. Even though there was no one on the beach but me, relatively far away from him. He had to traverse the space that separated him from the sea. He told me he would do it. He ran very quickly, all alone on the bare beach. On the smooth and sunlit beach where not a shadow moved except his own, long and slender. He ran with little steps, then walked awkwardly without turning around, his eyes riveted to the sea. Finally he reached it and hid himself in it.

I wouldn't have thought that man could swim with such a heavy and shameful body. But he took off quite easily on the surface of the water. After a turn, he passed in front of me. He looked at me and laughed. Between two breaststrokes he laughed and his face emerged from the water, resting on the water and exposed by his smile. No more shame in his agile body, and his mouth hung open. He was proud of how well he swam, so much so that he went far from the shore. I wondered why he was laughing and looking at me, he seemed to be making fun of himself. Perhaps it was because he loved swimming so much.

The sea was pretty rough, and soon I could see nothing of the man, neither his skull nor his feet. I followed him with my gaze for a brief moment as he advanced courageously toward the open ocean. Then, nothing.

It was too hot to sit tranquilly in the sun. I sprawled diagonally facing the sea, my head resting on my elbow. When I could no longer see the man, I let my head fall. That way I could better see the sea. It seemed greener. I didn't know what to do, and I placed my ear completely flat against the sand to listen. You hear nothing against the sand, you collide with a clogged silence. Against the ground you normally hear critters nibbling and roots bursting. Against the sand, nothing.

The waves arrived in regular rows before my eyes. Perpetually they arrived. I saw only them, the waves. Soon they were my breath, the beating of my blood. They visited my chest and left me, withdrawing, hollow and resounding like a cove. With the little beacon to the left now out, I could no longer see anything, neither the rocks nor the houses. I no longer had parents or a place to return to, I awaited nothing. For the first time I stopped thinking of Nicolas. I was at peace.

There was no one on the beach. No one had seen the man drown but me.

There was a very soft light over the sea. The sea was rising. The sun was no longer as warm. Night would arrive like an event, and I was waiting for it. It would arrive with its parade of stars and moons in a motionless straddling of the sea.

When it was dark, I thought I glimpsed the memory of the little black trace of the man's laugh near me. I pictured him: he had descended into the sea very slowly, cutting a straight path with the motionless sumptuosity of seaweed. He had shifted in a few minutes from extreme haste to extreme slowness.

There was a moment of total darkness. The sea was ink and it was cold.

I went back to the hotel.

. . .

It did happen, Jérôme's death, but Nicolas is also dead. Clémence is gone, Noël is abandoned. My parents have become quasi-insane, finished.

Something more could have happened to me, for example dying or losing Tiène (which amounts to the same thing). Obviously you could say that it's my fault. But how? In everything that's happened, I don't really see what role I played. Impossible not only to find the trace of remorse but to recognize in what happened what I wanted, what I didn't want, what I was expecting, what I wasn't expecting.

Nicolas on the train tracks: people didn't dare bring him to us. I went down with Tiène in the September dawn. Those three pieces of man had been my brother Nicolas. Difficult to imagine now that I hadn't always known he would die like that. How could I know? Is it really me who yelled and ran stupidly for hours around

Nicolas's body? Did I really manage to forget that he would die?

Only at this very minute can I consider myself without a smile. Even yesterday, I was the most naive. And I'm still just as naive today, even if differently, for believing myself to be any less naive. We leave that to take this. In winter, the naïveté of the summer; in the summer, the naïveté of the winter.

. . .

In two days I will leave here. I woke up late and came to the very end of the jetty, near the lighthouse. The sea is howling. The sun is nice. It's not cold. I'm not tired, but I have no desire to walk. I lie down on the dry sand against the dune, and I am still. Difficult to position one's body and one's head. The idea arrives, rambling like a drunk; it rolls you under it, ideas of Nicolas and Tiène.

I know how to escape them. I look at my knees or my breasts that lift my dress and immediately my thought curves and returns to me, obedient. I think of myself. My knees real knees, my breasts real breasts. An observation that counts.

I also came here to tirelessly contemplate my person. Among a thousand others, I am the one who grew within my mother's body and took the place that another could have occupied. I am simultaneously each one of those thousand others and those thousand others in one person. As much as you can imagine each of them, you can imagine that they are in fact me. They are as indefinitely replaceable as I know I am not, since it's always in relation to me that I imagine the ones who could have been in my place. That's my most minuscule and most reassuring definition. I am reduced to the very impossibility that I feel in thinking: at this moment another could be lying in my place by the sea, and it would amount to the same thing.

I see the little lighthouse a mile away. At night it illuminates the sea. I already know the lighthouse keeper, his wife, their child. The husband is at the wiretap at the top of the tower. His wife knits a stocking. The child sleeps. I could have been one of them. I have a real fascination with their existence. Same for the waitress at the hotel, and Dora, the madwoman of Ziès, and the Ziès cobbler who all year round in his shop makes shoes to walk in the plain of the Rissole.

Of course I've been awaiting some event since I arrived in T., probably the calm I'll feel when I know there is nothing left to wait for. Although I do the same thing here every day (invariably, I go to the sea from the hotel and from my room to the sea), I am sometimes joyful for no reason; sometimes, also for no reason, I am ablaze with a black sadness from the morning on. I am then forced to listen to all the bellowings of my desires.

I would like for the summer to be as perfect in me as it is outside, I would like to forget to be always waiting. But there is no summer of the soul. We watch the summer that passes before us while we remain in our own winter. We should abandon this season of impatience. Grow old in the sun of its desires. Since it's useless to wait when we are always waiting for something well beyond what we could hope for. To be amused, joyful, smooth, and beautiful to look at. To please Tiène like any other, always a new other. Since I would be no one.

If I could open myself up and cleanse myself of bitterness, of wind, of sea.

But my skin is sealed like a sack, my head hard, brimming with brains and blood.

. . .

It was the next morning that a fisherman found his clothes and brought them to the station. They knew right away where the man was staying because all the hotel records are sent to the station. They came to wake the owner early in the morning.

When I came down, everyone was talking about it. It was raining and people had nothing else to do. Though they knew nothing about his life, everyone had a lot to say about that man. He had arrived two weeks ago. It was his second time here. The maids remembered him. They said that he was a charming man, always happy and pleasant. I didn't remember him as a charming man; his face was severe, he said little, and most of the time among his acquaintances he was silent. But it's true that one can seem charming to an owner for these reasons alone.

Last year he'd come for twenty-one days. The maids counted: this time it had been fifteen, barely fifteen days because he'd died in the night. It was rather extraordinary that no one noticed he hadn't come back last night. What a shock it was to the owner in the morning when they brought her the clothes of one of her guests! All her other guests swarmed around her. A good number of people had drowned near here. They talked about them all, from the ones long ago to the ones last year, detailing their lives and their drownings. There were those that had been found, those that had never been found, those that were all alone, the elderly, the young, especially the young, it's such a shame. The guests had seen people disappear on all the beaches of France. Thus, in the space of half an hour, they had tallied a good twenty drownings. Then the conversation died out on its own and people began to watch the bad weather through the windows.

I waited twenty minutes for the maid to bring me my breakfast. I was in my usual corner. The sea was low and gray. In the haze, a small boat passed and disappeared.

I thought I would go to the beach early despite the rain. For fifteen days I had done only that, go to the beach, return to the hotel, then go back to the beach.

A few guests appeared around me. They recognized me from seeing me around. Every morning they asked about my health. I told them I was doing well. But they started up again each day. Since I was alone, maybe they assumed I was there because I was sick or to console myself over some misfortune.

One of them spoke to me of the drowned man with a slightly tender discretion, a lowered voice; he was a very young man with a red short-sleeved shirt and a polite tone. "You know, he actually asked me where you swam. I saw you going off to the left as usual, near the lighthouse, so I told him. I didn't know him, but he seemed timid and you yourself said nothing . . . I saw him go over there, he must not have found you . . ."

This young man was with a young blond woman who nodded her head as if to say: "Yes, yes, that's how it goes, that's how life goes, so silly, just as this young man is telling you . . ."

The man's clothes had been thrown haphazardly on the next table over, gray clothes with black stripes, their linings stained with rain and grime; their slightly swollen shapes recalled their lost movements. Everything had been removed from the pockets, the wallet and the papers thick and bloated with water that made the ink run. The man was named Henri Calot, he was a candy salesman, it was true; he had been married twice and had two children, Jeanine and Albert. Those papers reeked of accident, they smelled of wet paper thrown into streams, they exuded accident; everyone contemplated them in a stupor, how simple it was. People didn't want things to be so simple, so obviously simple. They surrounded the remains of the man, seething with passion, breathing in with their nostrils what that death might reveal of the ghastly and the reassuring.

The owner carefully enclosed the letters and photos in a brand-new envelope. She did it like someone who knows what she's doing. There was nothing left on the table except for his ID, swollen with that insipid drizzle that had been falling since yesterday, soaking the tiles and numbing these men with thoughts and laziness.

"You must not have seen him . . . ," the young man repeated.

I said yes, I had seen him. Everyone surrounded me because I was the last person in the world to have seen that man while he was still alive.

"You saw him swimming?" I said yes, I didn't think much of it. I said he had swum out in front of me.

So they stared at me. My soiled long-sleeved dress, my messy hair, my ruined hands, I saw, they stared. These details probably explained a lot. Around me were a dozen faces frozen with curiosity. I realized they were waiting for me to speak, and it was clear they weren't really understanding me: I hadn't said anything, no doubt I was just keeping to myself, but now I would really shock them, that's what they thought. I should have kept quiet. I found nothing to say and I felt myself blush. As I continued my silence, a more and more visible stain spread over their faces, the same expression that made them all resemble one another.

I should have kept quiet.

"You didn't see that he was drowning?" asked the owner, "You didn't understand . . . ?"

The sea was there, behind the windowpanes. I would have liked to disappear into it completely. If I had taken off, those people would have held me back.

I said that I didn't know, that in truth I hadn't seen the man drown exactly; at a certain point I hadn't seen him anymore, yes, but can we ever know, can we know that a man is drowning simply because we don't see him anymore? Maybe he had changed direction, maybe he was such a good swimmer that he had swum very far and I just couldn't see him. I hadn't looked for him, that was true, I hadn't followed him with my gaze, so the exact moment when he disappeared had escaped me.

"But why didn't you call for help? Why not?" I repeated that it would have been useless, that by the time I'd realized, he wasn't visible anymore, it would have been useless and anyway there hadn't been anyone on the beach but me and I wasn't a very strong swimmer.

"Why didn't you say anything? Do anything? Call out?" I repeated the same things, that it would have been completely useless, that when I had seen that man for the last time, he was swimming happily and I would have bothered him by sending someone after him. He was clearly a very strong swimmer and since he wanted to appear so to me (according to what the young man had said), I would have upset him by sending for help. Perhaps if I had, he would have struggled to swim and would have drowned in an even more terrible way, in the despair of displeasing me. I realized that perhaps none of this was making any sense, but I repeated it, it would have been useless to call out, there had been no one, absolutely no one on the beach but me, and I wasn't a very strong swimmer.

Those people were not satisfied with my explanations. It was as though I hadn't said anything, I kept having to repeat myself. They kept questioning me without listening to me, and I felt that no response would have been able to satisfy them.

I stopped responding. Those people, I didn't know them. And yet I felt flushed as though they were intimidating me. I forced myself to remain calm, to chase away that blood, that shame from my face. I left.

I walked one last time along the sea. As far as the eye could see, there was no one on the beach on the lighthouse side. A fine, icy rain was falling, the kind that chaps your lips, blurs your sight. The wind gathered it in bunches and threw it in my face, preventing me from walking, from breathing. This was not made for us, this complicit rain and wind, this depraved sea. The air was brutal and blowing in every direction, you couldn't nestle yourself in the wind and walk with it or even breathe it. It was suddenly missing from you, beneath your nose. It was worse than anger. A party to which you hadn't been invited.

I took shelter against a secluded rock and sat down. Suddenly I was elsewhere, in the distance. I felt better. My cheeks were cold now when I touched them. Bunches of rain carried by the wind passed over the rock but didn't reach me. My hands on my face smelled like the cold, I didn't recognize them anymore. I think I was sad. I cried. I wished I never had to leave that place, never again in my life. I cried because I had to leave.

. . .

Something was bound to happen to me. I waited for some event to surge up one morning that would heal me once and for all from the ridiculous wait my life had become since I'd arrived in T. But two weeks I've been here, and nothing has happened.

The owner told me earlier that she couldn't keep me here anymore after "yesterday's incident."

PART THREE

Nine at night at the Ziès train station and I didn't notify Tiène. It's raining and the night is pitch-black. On my way to Les Bugues (I'm counting): seventeen and fifteen, thirty-two days since Nicolas's death. Fifteen since I left for T. Those people were right to throw me out of the hotel. Since yesterday, it's been raining over the sea, here too, a fine mist put a stop to the wind and falls patiently, noiselessly. October is kneading the dough of winter. This will last for the full duration of the new moon; in fact, there it is now between thick branches of clouds slowly dispersing. They wanted nothing to do with me in T. because of that drowned man. Dozens drown every day, but I was there to see him. It's old news already, even though it was yesterday. The owner of the hotel had a scornful air about her. An air of duty. I was afraid. That they would figure me out. That I had done too much and they would discover who I was. That they could know who I was, say it. I thought of the poor murderers who learn so much about themselves, so much that they disgust themselves completely. She had a hefty chest, squeezed into a bra that was suffocating her. The tops of her breasts were hiked up into two swelling croissants. A redness on her throat, and her eyes avoided mine: "After what happened, I can't keep you here." Because I didn't call out: you're supposed to call out in these cases even when it's useless. Not that I didn't want to for a second or two. But it was calm, calm. In my stomach too and in my head, in that sun, nothing seemed to move. Not like in this moment now. Walking makes me think, and it occurs to me that this cold down my spine, it's fever. When Jérôme had a fever, he asked me for the notary. I will too, one day. That man drowned. I saw it, how a man drowns, I saw. It was calm, he drifted over the sea. The sea, in his arms, in his legs, gathered: even though I told him it was dangerous. He was drowning, but so far away, in a little image, in a corner of my eye that was still lit up by that big sun while everything else flickered in the shade. "You don't seem to see him, you see him, he's choking on the water that's tightening his chest and maybe he's watching you." It was quick, three minutes. I saw him, and I didn't see him anymore. "He drowned, that's all." I didn't lie to the other guests. That was all. Nothing to add. It's better than in your bed. To meet your end as you swim against the wind, at the crest of the waves. I know what he must have thought: "I don't have the time to die. Of course, I see that I must. But give me another few minutes so that I can take the time to die properly." In the noise, a noise from all sides, in the water, the water in my ears, the wind, the water, the noise, the senseless chaos, the chaos melded into chaos. "Give me a minute to lift my chest out of the water. After, I'll want to, after, yes, but first, breathe in a long, endless gulp of blue air. Let me die of breathing. After, after, yes, but before, I beg man and God! Oh please, a gasp of air, it's my right, my right to breathe one more time!" I recognize that all of this was happening somewhere, near me. It was nice out. Not like now. The rain will never end. When the bad weather starts in September, it lasts. No moon, at most we sense it but behind the thick sky. It's also lacking air, but on the other side of the rain, high up, the calm. Planes can pass through there. That's how they avoid the rain. It's Jérôme who told me that. I remember Jérôme. He would get up, stretch, and exercise in the courtyard. In the morning in Les Bugues. In the winter. It was nice out. We had just had coffee and felt it warming our stomachs as we went out in the cold. "To think there are people in offices wasting away at their desks, paying no mind to a day like this," Jérôme would say. He exercised to keep from growing old, all to die from a single blow. But then he didn't go to work, he went back inside to warm up. That's how I learned there are liars, people who take one step outside and do nothing more than say a few nice words. Praise the lovely day only to shut themselves inside to warm up. He lied, always lied. When I saw him, the day was waning; I remembered that it would fade and that the night would come like the day before. I remembered everything. I would avoid passing through the courtyard and skirted the outbuildings, but thinking about avoiding him exhausted me just as much as seeing him. But Nicolas, him, when I caught sight of him, it was quite different. His hair, his eyes, his teeth, shone intensely in the morning. He would approach me and smile, say that he was going to work down below: "Are you cold, Françou?" Next to him, Mâ dragged the empty plow. So much joy, so much, at seeing him again. With that face that was never entirely familiar. We never really spoke to each other. We always waited for the moment when we would speak, just the two of us. When we would say that we loved each other, that we liked each other. But only now could I have said it to him; now that he's dead and it's useless, I can. Before, I would never have dared. He stood upright, Nicolas, his chest was smooth and stuck out in the wind. Only at night would he think of Luce and turn sad. He was my brother. You only ever have one. Now he's dead, resting easy. The ground is warm in winter. Nicolas must be warm. He must still have his teeth. His eyes have popped. When I think about it, when I think about how his eyes have popped, his eyes violet like a secret, wet, blinking, his eyes that saw, his perfect eyes. When I think about it, ah! a heavy blow to the pit of the pit of my stomach, not one minute more will I be able to live without Nicolas. But it's rare, I never really think about it the way I just have. It's shameful even. But there is no shame. Everything is fine, anything that happens, even thinking of one thing or another. We must not be afraid of our thoughts, of anything. Now that he's dead, Nicolas, we can rest easy. We must no longer be afraid or ashamed. Now he is warm in the warm ground. It's Jérôme who explained that the ground is warm. He knew many things. Without a doubt, I owe a lot of my knowledge to him. We could have handled him differently. Listened to what he said. We never listened to him. We should have. The things he said seem right to me now, all the same, anyone could have said them. What he wanted was to be heard. And everyone despised him. At the table when he would say something, everyone pretended to eat voraciously. Even when it was just cabbage, which no one liked. He would purposely keep quiet a long time so that we would be surprised by his voice and listen. And he would say things in a way that he intended to be amusing, shocking. In the form of questions: "Do you know, Nicolas, how I got my first stripe in the war?" What he wanted was to please us, please only us. No one else interested him. Hatred, that's what it was. Impossible to find, to listen, to lodge one of his words in our heads. Especially at the table when Jérôme was eating, we hated him. I'm disgusted that we didn't listen to him more. Because he didn't work and because he voraciously ate the food we gave him. He's a dirty thief, we thought, and pleased with himself on top of it. I don't think he knew it, he was a thief without knowing it. If he were here, I would say something nice to him. I would explain to Nicolas. I should have told him. That no hatred ever lasts. That we have to listen to them, all of them, the liars too. Now he doesn't ramble anymore, he won't ramble anymore, won't ramble ever again. Had we listened to him just once. But no, not a single time. Clémence must have, I suppose. Just as well, thinking about it makes me happy. Another three kilometers to go. It's a long way. It's October now. There was last October. One night, we were in the courtyard, Maman said: "The days are starting to be very short, it's cold. Already." And Nicolas proposed going in to start a fire. The first fire of winter. Jérôme was there and in a corner Clémence was rocking Noël for the first time in October.

There would be the next October, and others. Always others. Still those three kilometers to go. If I saw the doctor from Ziès I would wave to him, he would stop, I would get in his car; it would be warm inside from the heat of the engine, suddenly. I would want to stay there for a long time. Want him to drive slowly and for these three kilometers to be slowly traveled. That way, these shivers down my spine would stop. Maybe I'll be sick once and for all. Two months in bed. I would be weak. Tiène would take care of me. In that case, I would take the bedroom overlooking the garden, there would be a fire in the chimney, I would put on my prettiest nightdress. The doctor. Who knows what he thinks of us, or what the neighboring farmers think. Since the deaths of Nicolas and Jérôme, the departure of Clémence and Noël, and my parents' madness. They know, without having come to Les Bugues. Everything is known. What they don't know is just how little I care about them. I would like to be resting easy in a warm place and no longer moving. For example, near the fire in the workshop, or naked against Tiène, without moving, in my bed. But tomorrow I won't be tired anymore, I'll have forgotten, I'll have to deal with the sharecroppers. The thought that new people are in Les Bugues, that it will begin again . . . It bores me. I'll have to tell them what to do. I've never known how. It must be more exhausting than working. Tomorrow, the day after tomorrow, start work again, always the same thing. There are people who are rich and others who are poor. I will always be poor. I have a body built for work, in good shape, in good health. There must be others right now: people who walk in the rain with a suitcase in their hand, hair in their face, old worn-out boots, and in their body, boredom. But also an ease in the boredom, in the rain. Working in the tobacco farms, at five in the morning, in the frost, despite green and cracked fingers. Deep down, it won't displease me to start again; I'm not tired. It's quite the opposite. Down below, the Rissole flows and a small white sparkling sun will rise. In the end, there are good days. Quickly, let the buds grow quickly, so that we can cut them in April. But no, no, there will be no more good days, I don't know why. In any case, what I want is to stop these shivers down my spine. I'm starting to notice them again, there's no escape. When I go back to thinking of something, I also think of how I'm thinking of it again. If I found an opening in the cliff to shelter me from the rain, I would wait there; there is one, a bit farther on before the bend. But if I stop, I'll be thoroughly cold. It's best to get to Les Bugues. I no longer feel like I'm walking; it's like breathing at the end. Better to get to Les Bugues as far as the cold goes. For the rest, I will never be at ease anywhere again, never well again, never while at work. I believe it at this very minute, there will be no more great days. But that's not true. As if I didn't know it was false. Tomorrow I will have forgotten. A shame to forget everything, but for the best. A shame but for the best, that's it exactly, I don't know how to think anymore. I don't know why, a shame but for the best: that's my last thought. The wind carried it off; it belongs to the wind now, like the last feather of a dead bird. Nothing left to think about now. Nothing. My head is fresh, suddenly empty. In my brain, it's like pouring rain. Let the wind carry this last thought down a path.

Tomorrow someone will crush it, in the morning, underfoot. There is no more room in my head except for the sound of my steps. I hear it clearly in the immense tunnel of my head, from all sides, from a farm and from here too, shlep, step, my step. It's my own step, I hear it clearly. I will listen to it intently, I will focus on it to arrive home more quickly. Pjrr . . . pjrr . . . pjrr . . . Two by two, or three by three, or four by four. I don't know which foot follows the other. Depending on whether I think of the left or the right, it's the left or the right. I'd have to know which foot I first walked on as a baby. That's the only way to know; otherwise it's cheating, of course. I watch one foot, then the other foot takes a step, but the one being watched also took a step. In the end I cover a lot of ground. Stubborn, legs. Well-built, like arms, mine are strong, I used to plow sometimes. Too bad there are sharecroppers, we'll no longer be able to do what we want. In the end, by trying to arrange everything, all Tiène has managed to do is poison my life with his sharecroppers. No more plowing or horsing around with Clément as we chop down a tree. But that's just nonsense, we still can. Just have to know how to go about it. This suitcase is heavy. It's pulling on my left arm. It's all my parents' fault for settling here. We've wasted our lives on this road, Nicolas and I, for a bag of coffee or a pound of salt. Once a week we went to the market, but it was too long a trip for what we needed to buy there. Now there's also the cemetery, we'll have to carry flowers to the late Jérôme and Nicolas. Two deaths at once, it's a lot after all. It's rare. I won't go often to bring them flowers; it's too far, I'll never have the courage. Still have the parents to take care of, to try to preserve. All the same, Maman was nice to embrace. Papa, it's not fair. I would still like to keep him so I can spoil him and he can read The Man with the Broken Ear *to me at night, like when I had scarlet fever. No one knows how good he is. Before they die, I would like to offer them a bit of happiness, make them good coffee and galettes; with some money, I could buy them a car, we could take them out all the time; they're so curious to look around, they wouldn't think of Nicolas anymore. It's true that Tiène plays music for them. But at night only, so all day long they wait in their bed for night to come. He must be playing the piano right now. I don't want to think about him. Tiène. In a few hours he'll be in my bed, cool and smooth. Soon, but it's so far away, never will I arrive in Les Bugues. What makes me suffer makes him happy: to be alive. He's figured out how to live comfortably. With ideas from his books and his head, he's figured out good reasons to be happy. He thought of everything, even the worst-case scenario, which is having one short year to live. He knows that he's young. And also that he's old. He knows that he's Tiène. And also looks like other creatures. He knows that he has to die. And lovingly embraces his death, with his two living arms. Inside his arms, ah! I could sleep like in a well of summer, because of my willingness to die. There, you can hear the clouds move, in the moss, so soft, in the nest of his arms. He tried in vain to believe in every god. So he was sad (this is what must have happened but I'm not exactly sure, I only know that there are people who cannot do without such things, and Tiène is one of them). Then he didn't choose any of them, and he became happy. It's precisely when he's happy that we understand he was once sad and worried about gods. Because not just anyone can become innocent, not just anyone can laugh, indiscriminately, about what's serious and what's not. When he sleeps, I know. His eyelids are violet and his mouth is drawn; in that moment, he remembers. His old defeats. His childhood already defeated. He's beautiful. But he's also very good and his intelligence is vast, you are inside: a wisp of straw on a river. No matter which side you view him from, he's the best of everything you've seen. He slips through your fingers like a fish. Like a fish. He always wants to set off on trips. If he told me where, I'd be disappointed. Let him leave, let him leave, he'll leave, he'll leave. Never will I make up my mind, about trips, about books. It would be a shame, lovely trips for me alone. My feet are warm and swollen in my wet shoes; I already have blisters on my heels but I don't feel them, tomorrow I'll feel them when they've burst. My hands: two heavy lumps at the ends of my arms. I'm heavy. All of my thoughts linger, stumble, merge. No idea chases away another. Disorder. Order too, each idea in its turn, there's no denying it, for example: I chose to remain in Les Bugues forever. Then immediately there wasn't a corner of the world where I had any desire to go. Laziness. I tell myself it's not worth it. That other people are better suited to leave. Then immediately I think no. That no one is better suited than me to leave. Once and for all I'd like to make up my mind. I'd like to choose to disgust myself. And be able to smile. I'd like to choose to love myself. And be able to smile. Yet she exists. She exists, the-one-I-love who delights me. For whom I have the tenderness that I have for everyone, anyone. I'd like to shelter her from my head. Find her, tame her, give her to Tiène. Give her beautiful children who will suckle her breasts. She would be set in spring. Ah! I want her to laugh, laugh, set in spring. I need to protect her from my damned head, old vicious head, old, old. The one I like defends herself. She has remained timid like the young women who have not yet been of use. Maybe they'll never take her out in the spring. Never. They'll lay her down, they'll place her next to the dead who are resting easy, nice and warm. If there were someone next to me, I'd tell them everything. To see if there are others. If there are many others like me or just one. Let him leave, Tiène. I wouldn't have any more pain. Nothing more will ever cause me pain, once he's left, I'd be able to rest easy. I'd no longer ask myself whether he's going to leave or not. Nice and warm in the workshop. I wish I could already have arrived in Les Bugues so I could start right away, right away, for life. Sit next to the fire for life. I'd stay there, I'd never forget this night. All the same, sometimes I'd die willingly. It's as though I were discovering that I am still young. The dead, they're everywhere, lying in the cool and warm cemeteries. I will too, one day. Lie with my side part in my hair and my scar on my left hand. The one I got while trying to carve a whistle for Nicolas out of an elderberry branch. A long time ago. But it won't fade. On my dead hand, it will remain. Henceforth hidden. No one will know. I'd like to stop thinking. This road is long. Why Les Bugues? I'd like to leave here forever and stay at the same time. Forget the arrangement of copper pots in the kitchen, forget to polish them Saturday afternoon. Because I'd like to have nothing left that still brings me pleasure. I'd like to be the most alone. I am the most abandoned. The heaviest, with my thoughts. Even though they're chaotic, I manage. I'm used to it. Already I recognize them each time, each one with its little mouse face. There will be no more new thoughts. We'll have the easy life. I've been around my head. It's the heaviest. No one knows it. I am the most pitiful, like everyone, the most pitiful. I don't care about being the most pitiful, the least pitiful. We'll have the easy life, yes we will. I love the rain. I just have to extend my face and open my mouth. I like that people are dead, I like these shivers down my spine. My blisters on my heels, I love them. All my stories. We'll have the easy life. Ah! there's the Ziès cemetery. Where little Nicolas and old Jérôme sleep. I didn't love Nicolas enough, never enough. I should have looked after him, cared for him more. It's been a century since he returned to death. I wish I could kiss the empty space of his eyes. Sniff them, his hollow eyes, until I recognize my brother's scent. It would do me good, warm me up, make me young. Alas, past the cemetery, Nicolas becomes smaller and smaller in my mind and the road is long after the cemetery. All the same, his warm eyes. The wind is cold, and without my brother I turn back into an old vagabond in the wind, the wind itself, an old vagabond. Nicolas again. I always think back to Nicolas. Sometimes I want to swear aloud but it would be useless, I'll always think back to him, again and again. He's dead. It happened thirty-two days ago, and now he no longer needs to die; all is silent. Never again will he die. It's done.*

—And me, walking, adding days to days since his death, without wanting to, without being able to do otherwise. Because

I don't want to die. Already thirty-two days have passed that he hasn't seen, autumn so red, so porous with rain, with mud. And I walk, I don't know why, what's still expected of me. What they want me to do tomorrow. No, nothing is truly closed off to someone who is not yet dead. I'll have my place in tomorrow too. Whether I want it or not. And where exactly I will be led through the days and the days, I don't know. I could try to stop here in the rain and refuse to keep moving, but it would be useless. There would still be a place for me, a kind of place. If Nicolas had thought of that, he wouldn't have bothered to suffer for Luce or bothered to kill himself. He was a little fool. But I wish I could embrace him. Ah! to hold him tight once and for all. I'm old. Because I can no longer embrace him, I'm old with all my future years. Since that trip to T. I'm sure of it. All these tragedies and then that man who drowned. I overwhelmed myself with tragedy, it broke out everywhere, from all sides. And I'm to blame. At least you might think that, but I, I know that it doesn't matter to me. There's nothing to do about boredom, I'm bored, but one day I won't be bored anymore. Soon. I'll know that it's not even worth the trouble. We'll have the easy life.

. . .

It felt as if I was returning from Ziès as usual, after running a few errands. Except that now I was going to see Tiène again and meet the new sharecroppers. Though my suitcase was light, I was tired, I was hungry as I approached Les Bugues. But if the road had been longer, I could have kept walking all night long, I could have done it, as long as I was still just as hungry and warm, still listening to the same soft crunch of my wet shoes on the road.

It was after the intersection, about halfway home, that I heard the piano. That's right, at this hour, Tiène plays in the workshop. It must be warm and bright with light in there.

I can already picture Tiène's back, his neck, the profile he'll turn my way when I enter. He'll rise but won't come to meet me. His hands will leave the piano and fall along his upright, motionless body. Maybe he's changed his mind. Who knows? Maybe he's decided to want what it means to stay rather than what it meant to leave. With the same incomprehensible stubbornness. Who knows?

I sat on the embankment. The music reached me at the same time as the wind, there on my shoulders.

I was comfortable in my wet, warm clothes.

The rain is no longer important. Close by, it's a precise sizzling, far away an enormous stamping.

It bores me to arrive straightaway, now that I'm here.

There's no escaping Tiène, I know. I'll be the one he wants, the most terrible, the best. I'll be beautiful if he wants. I'll do my hair. I'll wear the red dress with the gray flowers. I don't mind. On Sundays we'll bring flowers to Nicolas. That's right, Nicolas . . . But after everything? We'll put our little boy in Nicolas's room. But we'll have to repaint it white. It'll be up to Tiène to decide. Me, I don't mind.

Someone moves on the path. I recognize him, it's Clément with his lantern.

He stopped and sat down on the embankment next to me: "Mademoiselle has returned?" I asked him what was new. He told me that Mr. Tiène still played the piano every night in front of Mr. and Mrs. Veyrenattes and Mademoiselle Barragues. How long had she been back? Ten days. "She came back to fetch something she had left here when Nicolas was still around and has come back every night since."

Clément knows things the moment they happen, the winters, the rains, the frosts, the children, the deaths. He doesn't prefer anything to anyone, anyone to anything. He is careful not to have an opinion, they call him old, call him stupid, he does neither good nor harm. From the top of his hill, he sees it all: on this day he leaves his winter coat behind, on that day he puts it back on. I've always wondered what he thinks about for months on end while he tends to his flock. I believe he doesn't feel that he is living out a man's life; his thoughts wake with the day and wane with the evening, they follow his sheep, they cling to his hands as they milk udders, they watch over his fire.

We didn't speak for a long time. Really, there is nothing to say to Clément. Well, how were the new sharecroppers? According to Mr. Tiène, they were the right kind of people. Nothing had happened, the lambs had been sold, the wool too, no illnesses, it was almost time to pen the animals for the winter. And were the parents still as unreasonable as they had been since Nicolas's death? Clément hadn't noticed. Madness is like reason, reason like madness. All it takes is spying on madness without the spirit of reason and it explains itself on its own, makes itself understood. No, he hadn't noticed a thing. The other morning he had seen Papa, who had seemed to him the same as always. Where, and what had he told him? Well, it was near the railroad embankment, near the Rissole, very early. They had chatted a moment. Mr. Veyrenattes had said it was very nice weather for October and that it was good to see the sunrise. Clément didn't remember him saying anything unreasonable. As for Mrs. Veyrenattes, no one saw her in the Les Bugues courtyard anymore. Clément hadn't asked Mr. Veyrenattes about her because he understood that she had been suffering since Nicolas's death. (With this, he stops talking. He knows: you have to wait for the pain of a child's death to pass, like the pain of a child's birth; the right amount of time has not yet passed.)

However, walking through the courtyard, he had glimpsed her through the window, lying on her bed. She had waved at him.

I see her: she's traveling, she sails on a sea of pain. She cannot yet stop but gives a gentle wave to let the others know that she hasn't forgotten them, even though she is so far away it might seem like she doesn't notice them crossing the courtyard. They leave her alone and she is grateful for that and feels affection toward them. She probably feels bad for not being there to oversee the courtyard, but she can't help it, she has things to think about: this Nicolas who won't come home again and whose hair she wishes she could caress.

Clément has stopped talking. In the gleam of the lantern, I see his summer coat covered in a fine plumage of rain. His eyes are lowered, and in the shadow of his cap, his face reveals none of its features, nor does it look like itself, only some shiny wrinkles that give the impression of a halted unending old age. He will not wrinkle any further, he will not speak another word. Within Clément, it's Time that is near me.

I told him that I would follow him to his cabin and sleep there.

We climbed up the hill of Ziès. He offered me his straw mattress, he made a fire, and together we ate some bread and cheese. At one point we heard the trot of Luce Barrague's horse. I went out on the doorstep. The windows of Les Bugues overlooking the courtyard were lit.

. . .

The next day and the two days that follow, I stay with Clément. I'm a little sick; I caught a cold on the way back from Ziès.

Clément makes me a fire, he prepares me something to eat and then tends to his sheep. He goes each night to

Les Bugues, he comes back late, I don't ask him what's going on there and he doesn't say a thing either.

I have no desire to leave my hiding place, without knowing exactly why. I have a fever and I sleep almost all the time. When I open my eyes, I see my body wrapped up in Clément's brown blanket and, through the open door, the valley of the Rissole, bleak, under a sky of smoke. The rain falls in irregular intervals and fills the space between the sky and the valley with a shining vapor. The fire burns more or less intensely depending on the time of day. In the morning it's red, in the evening it's pink beneath the white ashes. The cabin has only one window that looks onto the forest. Nothing on the wall but a rifle. There's a bitter odor of curdled sheep's milk, mixed with the oozing scent of wet logs piled up on each side of the fireplace. After the downpour, the scent of rain enters and licks the walls of the cabin, bathes in the scent of the milk and the fire. This third scent is the scent of my most perfect solitude. I know it without thinking. I inhale it all the way to its most ancient depths, a thing open and dispersed that is now closed again. Nothing can be heard but the nibbling of the fire. My eyes fix on the Rissole and close.

Clément enters. He looks like one of the trees before autumn. He makes the fire, takes a pipe, and sits for a moment on the straw mattress across from my own. Then he goes off again. Without saying a thing, without even looking at me. And yet he knows I'm lying here, in this bed.

When the first lamps are lit, I always hear the steps of Luce Barrague's mare. The mare makes her way up slowly. It's true that the slope is steep. I see her: enshrined in a large rain hood, ever more beautiful, coming for Tiène. Tiène despite the rain, the wind, the shame. What shame she must feel. A thousand mountains couldn't stop her. Her mare would die there, she would grow old there, she would grow old just to arrive there, nothing would stop her but me. To the swaying gait of her mare, I fall back asleep.

I am too busy feeling exhausted. At first I feel too hot. Then a sweat exudes from all of my skin and leaves me cool, stiff with coolness. This fever is sweet, sweet. It's like the sweet rain that always comes and goes in this season. The next winter will soon begin.

I sleep. Whatever they may be, the events to come won't make me happy or sad. I will flow through them, I have chosen my place, which is here where there is nothing to do but watch.

If only I would show myself. Luce would run off, Tiène would be caught off guard by my return. I will never again be able to stand that, because of me, people feel shame. And explain to them, no; explain to them that my shame is greater than theirs, the shame of provoking theirs, no. I'm glad that Luce's mare goes forth carrying such a beautiful girl. That the lights go on, that Tiène sits down at the piano and Papa and Maman come listen to the music soon after.

Luce. How afraid she must feel at the thought of my return. How timid she must feel suddenly faced with herself as she sees herself return to Les Bugues and sit down in the workshop with Nicolas's parents. I like that Luce's desire goes so far as to conquer her courage. That she advances toward Les Bugues with desire as her only weapon, abandoned by her cowardly courage, her cowardly remorse. I like that Tiène is desired in this way, that Tiène is the object of such desire. I like a world in which such paroxysms of oblivion can exist. Luce has returned.

I know that my parents, whose discretion could come across as guilt, are always polite with Luce. Oh! and how I adore Papa, who would be angry at himself for being angry at Luce, Papa who may still be unhappy at the thought that she might suspect him of this anger. Because, after Nicolas's death, if he can stand himself, he has to stand Luce and the thought that Luce had something to do with it.

Around ten at night, Clément returns. We eat together happily, without saying a thing. We are gluttonous only for sheep cheese and milk soup. After dinner, the icy smell of the stars enters the cabin. It's good to be at Clément's.

. . .

The first sunny day, I have to go back down to Les Bugues. We go out when the weather is good. What I prevented from happening I can no longer prevent because Tiène must be aware I'm at Clément's. When the sun rises, Tiène will go to the terrace and feel joyful. His first thought will be this or that or about going away in the winter. And he will no longer change his mind. I have never hindered or prevented him from doing what he desired. He will do what he wants.

Three days, three nights, have gone by. Clément never mentioned calling the doctor. He kept saying I needed warmth and sleep.

The first sunny day has arrived after an overnight shower. Clément opened the door and the window facing the woods, all the way. I felt cured. You shouldn't try to stay here. I got up. Clément lent me his hooded cape and I went down to Les Bugues.

The path was muddy, already a winter mud, red with leaves. From the woods, the wind came in clean, youthful angles. Yes, I was completely cured.

On my way, I noticed Tiène in the courtyard. He was speaking to the sharecroppers and seemed to be giving them orders. He was wearing a dark suit and seemed smaller than when I had left him. Seeing him made me remember. It's true, we loved each other. At that instant, I started to desire Tiène again. During my fifteen days in T. I hadn't thought about it, but at that moment, I watched him and each of his gestures reminded me, through his very indifference, of the more secret ones I knew.

I wondered why he was giving orders to the sharecroppers. He had chosen them and moved them in when I should have been the one to do it since I was the only mistress of Les Bugues. But with Tiène, you could never be sure.

When I arrived, he was in the living room. He had probably seen me arrive. He wasn't doing anything. He was smoking and, his hand under his chin, staring out the window. He hardly turned his head, I could see only his profile.

"I know that you've been at Clément's for three days." How did he know? The Ziès doctor had come to visit the sharecropper's son and had seen me as I got off the train and passed through the village. How did he know I was at Clément's? He had guessed. Where else could I have been but there, at that old fool's house?

I felt like laughing, I don't know why, but I was scared of upsetting him. I told him I was going to eat lunch and get ready and that after, if he wanted, we could go see the sharecroppers. I had never seen Tiène angry, seized by a real childish anger. I imagined how he had gotten there, slowly at first, then all of a sudden, with all of his strength, without delay. That was probably what made me want to laugh.

I know he's staying now. Reluctantly, reluctantly, no doubt. But he's staying. I got him without wanting to keep him. I have him. So Tiène was this man who, in the end, would stay.

There was a lot to do in the house. I prepared lunch and went to see what work had to be done.

Later that morning, I went to see the parents. They were still in bed. When they saw me, they smiled and said they were becoming quite lazy. Maman said that she was tormented over Nicolas and Noël and that she wanted them to come back. Papa said that he would return to work the next day, that one couldn't always be resting.

I stayed with them for a moment. Papa appeared to be thinking. Maybe he wondered where I'd come from. Maman's eyes shifted from the courtyard to me, from her hands to the courtyard. Her gaze became indiscreet, it settled on you and stared at you with an empty intensity. They probably hadn't been very well taken care of in my absence. Their pajamas are gray, their sheets too. Because of the open window, there's still enough light in the room. Their big hands lie pell-mell in the bed, their arms bare up to the elbows, their hair tangled, their forms absent. They have lost even their parental scent. There is no consolation, there is no longer enough flesh to embrace. You can no longer embrace them.

Papa got dressed. We brought Maman out to the front door and settled her into a chair in the sun. I whispered in her ear that Tiène and I would soon be married and she would have grandchildren. She raised her hands several times and let them fall back down on her knees. "She's getting married, Louis; they're getting married!" And Papa seemed joyful. They asked me to explain how it had happened. I told them that it had been decided a while ago but that we had kept it hidden to surprise them.

I only saw Tiène again late in the afternoon. Until then I stayed in the workshop by the fire. At night, I brought Maman in; she wanted to walk around the house and she even made coffee in the kitchen for the first time in over a month. She ran into Tiène, who had gone to fetch wood, and I heard her ask him when our wedding would be.

Tiène returned to the workshop. He asked me what I had said to Maman and I repeated it to him. He turned halfway around, lit by the gleam of the fire. It's true that, seven months ago, as I watched Tiène, who wasn't speaking, I had suspected the silent and unattainable order of the world. He told me I was pale and thin. And also: "We'll get married quickly, because I have to be off again before the winter."

Tiène took me around the left wing of Les Bugues. He took me by the waist in a corner of the large living room. He told me: "You'll also have to become kind and beautiful." And he smiled along with me. The two of us, we knew why.

We heard Luce's horse coming up, as precise as the hour itself. It was ten o'clock. It had to be done: Tiène asked me to wait, and he went to tell her about our marriage.

When he returned, we excused ourselves. I was tired. I wanted to have dinner and for us to go up to my room together. I wanted to sleep with him. He approached me and put my face against his neck, he squeezed it very tight, he hurt me. I didn't ask him a thing. He told me he hadn't even been able to touch Luce Barragues because I was the one he wanted.

It was dark out, an October night, fresh from the storm.

TRANSLATORS' NOTE

The Easy Life is broken into three distinct parts that represent the three distinct stages of Francine Veyrenatte's coming-of-age. The first part, on the family farm in Les Bugues, is contained: it is the wave about to break. "Chaos, boredom, chaos." Like the structure of the sea, the calm between the waves. The style is contained in the same way the whole family, but especially its daughter, Francine, is imprisoned. Everyone in the household is simmering, about to boil over. You can feel the Veyrenattes, described by Francine as "dreamers and degenerates," pushing against their own individual walls, straining to break out of the sinister swamp of boredom keeping the family trapped in Les Bugues. The stifling atmosphere in Les Bugues is so intense that the tiniest thing can set off an explosion. And that's precisely what Francine does.

As we were translating part one, we were struck by the cruelty and coldness of Francine's prose as she describes Jérôme's excruciating, slow death. There is a detachment, almost a woodenness to the language that feels so different from a book like "Summer 80," which we co-translated together for the collection *Me & Other Writing*. There is none of the ethereality of her writing about love, writing, or the sea. We were drawn to staccato, monosyllabic vocabulary. The harshest-sounding word of all the choices for a given phrase. Hot instead of warm. Chaos instead of disorder. Boring instead of dull. Words like drag and scrape. Fat tears for *grosses larmes*. "Night cracks all over." "He smelled like hot hay." "My skin is sealed like a sack, my head hard, brimming with brains and blood." Through such alliteration, perhaps you can feel Francine's anger, her resentment, her clawing at the "dreamskin" of Les Bugues. You can predict the rupture that will come too. But Francine's syntax remains very in control in part one. You can almost feel Duras's attempts to impose order over her own internal chaos through her writing. Unlike her later works, there is less meandering, less pondering, less grasping at big questions and more urgency. It is as though she's under threat, writing as an attempt to fight back against some premonition, rather than an opportunity to reflect, relive.

But there is also a current running through this book that is present in her later work—a young woman's premonitory feeling of age, of fatigue, of already being ruined, *old with all my future years*, similar to the narrator of *The Lover*. The way we women who have lived too much life carry it around with us, all that has passed and all that we feel is still to come. And Duras shows us that it's not as simple as equating the old with boredom and ease, death with the calm after the storm. Life and youth and chaos are not so intrinsically bound either. There is a certain fluidity between these concepts. Francine describes her brother Nicolas as "aged with all the ages he had been in succession." Chaos, boredom, life, death, old age, youth: everything coexists in a mess as sticky as the end of August, reeking of rot. It's all connected. As translators, we have to make it all coexist, too. In Duras's work, each word seems to carry more than one meaning, resounding both with the preceding text and the text to come. Stylistically, she's a bit like August. She contains everything. Francine and her family are accumulating ages and fatigue, they are rotting and about to burst, about to become something new.

Francine fears waking up one day to find she has done nothing significant with her life, to find that she has never taken hold of her existence, never harnessed the force within her to do . . . something, anything. "I heard time gnaw at us like an army of rats," Francine says. This notion resonated very strongly with the two of us as we were translating. Even though we are by all accounts still young women with our lives ahead of us, we have both felt terrified by the possible lives that are slipping away, the clock ticking, doors closing, rats chomping. We became friends and later co-translators because of our mutual connection to Duras's work, the way we felt she ran through our blood and brains. Like Francine we feel ancient, and it scares us to think that all of that life heaped up in us could have been the wrong life. As we make decisions that inevitably block off certain paths and take us further away from the versions of ourselves we once imagined, it leaves a mark that we see in the mirror. As Francine says, "Once you lose the ability to forget, you are permanently deprived of a certain life." And in some ways, is that not also what translation is like? You choose words, and in doing so keep the text from becoming "a thousand times different" from what it could have been. With this translation, we had to pin down a version of the text, a version of Francine, who is also confronted with all her possible selves in part two, and must choose which one to go back home with.

If the first part of the book is a contained space, a house, the second is an infinite sea. In the wake of tragedy on the family farm, Francine travels to the coastal city of T. In the sea's infinite mirror, Francine is reflected an endless number of times, to the point where she no longer recognizes herself. She is overwhelmed, assaulted by all her possible selves. Soon after she arrives, she stares at her reflection in the hotel room mirror and watches herself dissolve. The mirrored armoire opens like Pandora's box, unleashing the selves Francine has never become, nor even dared to imagine. In that moment, Duras and Francine are unleashed in a dissociative crescendo that takes us all the way to Francine's elemental realization: "I am flower." *Je suis fleur,* it is one of those jarring, prophetic statements we knew had to be equally strange in English.

Duras must take Francine to the sea to find her, but first she has to lose her. And she does so through radical stylistic, structural, and grammatical twists. What grounded us through this section was Duras's voice, her inescapable rhythm, the way she makes use of repetition, her idiosyncratic shifts in perception and Delphian sentences. Here, that voice seems to be blooming for the very first time in the book's pivotal moment. The disconnect between who she always thought herself to be and the new self she finds there by the sea creates a violent split, a fragmenting of her inner being. As Francine stares at herself in the mirrored armoire and considers the many versions of herself, the pronouns, tense, and voice change from sentence to sentence, even within sentences:

Là, dans ma chambre, c'est moi. On croirait qu'elle ne sait plus que c'est d'elle qu'il s'agit. Elle se voit dans l'armoire à glace; c'est une grande fille qui a des cheveux blonds, jaunis par le soleil, une figure brune. Dans la chambre, elle tient une place encombrante. De la très petite valise ouverte, elle tire trois chemises pour avoir l'air naturel devant celle qui la regarde.

"Here, in my room, it's me. It's as if she no longer knows it's her. She sees herself in the mirrored armoire; she's a tall girl with blonde hair, yellowed by the sun, a tan face. In the bedroom, she takes up too much space. From the very small open suitcase, she pulls out three blouses to look natural before the girl watching her."

In French, Francine moves from "moi" to the impersonal "on" to "elle" to "une grande fille" to "celle qui la regarde." In English, she flits from "me" to the passive "it's as if" to "she" to "a tall girl" to "the girl watching her." The reader is watching Francine's unraveling happen in real time as she dissociates from herself, unable to identify as "me." It is meant to be jarring, confusing, obscure. What is the right pronoun? What is the key to this switching, the pattern to the fragmentation? Who is the right version of her? As translators, we want to replicate the disorder, the confusion, the abrupt changes and splinterings—but for us it comes with the risk of being seen as clumsy, or, worse, as too calculated, too in-control, because we have to make a specific choice at every turn.

We quickly saw that there was a pattern, some sort of evolution with how Duras was using the word "on" from the first part of the book to the third. "On," which can either be translated as "we," "you," "one," or in the passive voice, seemed to indicate Francine's shifting sense of self and power. In the first part, we translated "on" primarily as "we" to signify the shared Veyrenattes malediction. But in the second part, "on" starts to become tricky, to operate as a more radical, existential pronoun. As Francine unravels in her hotel room, Duras uses it as such: "I am not responsible for this age or for this image. You recognize it. [*On la reconnaît.*] It must be mine." Here, the psychological fragmentation of the character is reinforced through our choice to translate "on" as "you," as if Francine is addressing another her, another girl. However, it could easily have been translated as the passive "It is recognizable" or the impersonal "One recognizes it." The use of "you" reinforces Francine's inability to pin herself down. There are two, perhaps more, Francines in the room. A few lines later, she reaffirms this splitting: "I can't even hold myself in my arms [. . .] I wish I could embrace the girl that I am and love her," signaling directly to that "on," that "you," but in the third person. This "on" shadows Francine throughout her entire stay in T. Just lines before pronouncing "I am flower," she shifts to this "on" again: "I traveled to the hot and muddy vestibules of the earth that spat me out from its depths. And now I've arrived. You come to the surface. [*On vient à la surface.*]" It's as that "you," that "on," that Francine emerges, one of the sea's hatchlings, identifying the version of herself that will return to Les Bugues. As Francine loses sight of herself in part two, Duras finds her voice as a writer, and as her translators, we get to find it along with her.

At the start of part three, in the italicized interior monologue preceding her return to the family farm, the pronoun "on" makes another meaningful appearance. *On l'aura la vie tranquille,* "We'll have the easy life." It's repeated four different times and is what the monologue ends on, giving way to Francine's recovery. On her feverish walk, she chants it to herself like a mantra, an affirmation to give her the strength to make it home. In French, "on" resounds here as a general "we," not unlike part one, though this time, Francine is addressing all of her selves before she reaches home and they merge into a more decisive "I." After this stream of monologue, once everything eases, "on" mostly disappears. The past no longer seems to hang over Les Bugues like a collective curse; by going to T., she has moved beyond it somehow, and the self has been rendered whole. The book's ending is calm. Francine has a voice, a body, a purpose. Francine can have "the easy life" because she is fully herself now, has found her place in the world, and therefore is less erratic, less brimming with brains and blood and boredom and chaos.

The easy life in this book seems to be a marriage, a nuclear family, crawling back into her cage on the farm with her lover Tiène. Francine has learned the full scope of her force in T., but has decided to bury it in Les Bugues. Perhaps the easy life is resignation, return, holding your power at bay within you. And you can only "choose" the easy life when there is another path to take—a more difficult but more exciting and violent life. Whatever it may be, there is a sense that even if Francine appears to choose this easy life, her wild lifeforce will tear through the dreamskin again before long.

At the end of the book, the reader is left wondering: Has Francine fallen in love with Tiène, or with herself, through Tiène? He occupies her field of vision and then she remembers—oh, it's me I'm looking at, through him. It's me I'm thinking about, through him. He is just another mirror, like the sea, there for her to better understand herself and her power. He's all she has, out there in Les Bugues. So she has to use him, not let him slip away before she has a chance to know herself. This book bears witness to Francine's unraveling, but it is also about Francine amassing her force. As the novel closes, Francine is the one in control. She decides when she and Tiène will get married, she decides when the sharecroppers will reap the fields. She is the head of the household now—not her father, not Tiène, not Nicolas. No small feat for a woman.

There are many possible translations for the word "tranquille" in the title *La vie tranquille*, but we were quickly convinced by *The Easy Life* for our rendition. "Easy" kaleidoscopes in our translation, hum-drumming the reader into a worrisome ease, which, like Duras's "écriture courante," always seems to break into chaos. We ride that current with her, we are prey to the swell and swelling with words. They are Duras's words, but by way of that strange force that writes and that strange force that translates, they are Francine's and ours, also.

As we translated this book, our word choices had to be cohesive, yet amorphous. Our lines had to always be just about to take shape, on the point of becoming. We had to leave Francine open to multiple readings—even as we made choices as translators, our words had to be prismatic in their precision. We channeled Francine's boredom, her chaos, her youth and inherent old age. We let ourselves feel her fatigue, her containment, and her fragmentation, in turns. That's how you translate Duras: you become one of her dreamers and degenerates.

A NOTE ON THE AUTHOR AND TRANSLATORS

MARGUERITE DURAS was one of France's most important writers. Among her seminal works were *Hiroshima Mon Amour* and the international bestseller *The Lover,* which won the Prix Goncourt. She was born in Saigon in 1914 and died in Paris in 1996.

EMMA RAMADAN is a literary translator of poetry and prose from France, North Africa, and the Middle East. She is the recipient of a Fulbright, an NEA Translation Fellowship, the 2018 Albertine Prize, and the 2020 PEN Translation Prize.

OLIVIA BAES is a Franco-American multidisciplinary artist who grew up between France, Catalonia, and the United States. She holds a Master of the Arts in Cultural Translation from the American University of Paris.